Sandra Cis 

VINTAGE **CISNEROS**

Sandra Cisneros is a novelist, poet, short story writer, and essayist whose work gives voice to working-class Latino and Latina life in America. Her lyrical, realistic work blends aspects of "high" and popular culture.

Her novel *The House on Mango Street* (1984), a series of vignettes told from the perspective of a young girl growing up in Chicago, won the Before Columbus Foundation's American Book Award in 1985. This book has become a staple in school curriculums across the country.

Woman Hollering Creek and Other Stories (1991), a collection of short stories, won the PEN Center West Award for Best Fiction of 1991, the Quality Paperback Book Club New Voices Award, the Anisfield-Wolf Book Award, and the Lannan Foundation Literary Award, was selected as a noteworthy book of the year by *The New York Times* and *The American Library Journal*, and was nominated Best Book of Fiction for 1991 by the *Los Angeles Times.*

Cisneros is the author of three volumes of poetry: *Bad Boys* (1980), *My Wicked Wicked Ways* (1987), and *Loose Woman* (1994). Her other works include *Hairs/Pelitos* (1994), a children's book, and a novel, *Caramelo*, published in English and Spanish in 2002.

In 1995, Cisneros was awarded the MacArthur Foundation Fellowship. Other literary honors include a Texas Medal of the Arts, 2003; two fellowships, in fiction and poetry, from the National Endowment for the Arts, 1982, 1987; an honorary Doctor of Letters from the State University of New York at Purchase, 1993, and Loyola University of Chicago, 2001; the Roberta Holloway Lectureship at the University of California, Berkeley, 1988; the Chicano Short Story Award from the University of Arizona, 1986; the Texas Institute of Letters Dobie-Paisano Fellowship, 1984; an Illinois Artists Grant, 1984; and an artist residency at the Foundation Michael Karolyi, Vence, France, 1983.

Cisneros' books have been translated into many languages including Chinese, Danish, Dutch, French, Galician, Greek, Italian, Japanese, Korean, Norwegian, Serbian, Spanish, Swedish, Thai, and Turkish. Her work has been featured in major periodicals including *The New York Times*, *Los Angeles Times*, *The New Yorker*, *Glamour*, *Elle*, *Ms.*, *Story*, *Grand Street*, and *The Village Voice.*

Born December 20, 1954, in Chicago, Cisneros received her B.A. (1976) from Loyola University and her M.F.A. from the University of Iowa (1978). She has worked as a teacher to high school dropouts, a poet-in-the-schools, a college recruiter, an arts administrator, and as a visiting writer at a number of universities across the country.

Sandra Cisneros currently earns her living by her pen. She is nobody's mother, nobody's wife, and shares a home in San Antonio, Texas, with the love of her life.

BOOKS BY SANDRA CISNEROS

Bad Boys

The House on Mango Street

My Wicked Wicked Ways

Woman Hollering Creek

Loose Woman

Hairs / Pelitos

Caramelo

VINTAGE CISNEROS

Sandra Cisneros

VINTAGE BOOKS
A Division of Random House, Inc.
New York

A VINTAGE ORIGINAL, JANUARY 2004

"Hairs," "My Name," "Our Good Day," "Those Who Don't," "Darius & the Clouds," "The Family of Little Feet," "Hips," "Elenita, Cards, Palm, Water," "Four Skinny Trees," "No Speak English," and "A House of My Own" were originally published in *The House on Mango Street,* copyright © 1984 by Sandra Cisneros (Arte Público Press, 1984). "Preface," "Abuelito Who," "My Wicked Wicked Ways," "Ass," "Peaches—Six in a Tin Bowl, Sarajevo," and "14 de julio" were originally published in *My Wicked Wicked Ways,* copyright © 1987 by Sandra Cisneros (Third Woman Press, 1987). Reprinted by permission of the publisher. "Eleven," "Salvador Late or Early," "Tepeyac," "Never Marry a Mexican," "Bread," "Eyes of Zapata," and "Little Miracles, Kept Promises" were originally published in *Woman Hollering Creek,* copyright © 1991 by Sandra Cisneros (Random House, Inc., 1991). "You Bring Out the Mexican in Me," "You Like to Give and Watch Me My Pleasure," "Love Poem for a Non-Believer," "I Am So Depressed I Feel Like Jumping in the River Behind My House but Won't Because I'm Thirty-Eight and Not Eighteen," "Night Madness Poem," "I Am on My Way to Oklahoma to Bury the Man I Nearly Left My Husband For," "Cloud," *"Tú Que Sabes de Amor,"* "Mexicans in France," and "Loose Woman" were originally published in *Loose Woman,* copyright © 1994 by Sandra Cisneros (Alfred A. Knopf, 1994). "Verde, Blanco, y Colorado," "Chillante," "Mexico Next Right," "Tarzan," "So Here My History Begins for Your Good Understanding and My Poor Telling," "Cuídate," "Spic Spanish?," "All Parts from Mexico, Assembled in the U.S.A. or I Am Born," "The Vogue," "Someday My Prince Popocatépetl Will Come," and "Pilón" were originally published in *Caramelo,* copyright © 2002 by Sandra Cisneros (Alfred A. Knopf, 2002).

Library of Congress Cataloging-in-Publication Data
Cisneros, Sandra.
Vintage Cisneros / Sandra Cisneros.
p. cm.
ISBN 1-4000-3405-1
1. Hispanic Americans—Literary collections. I. Title.
PS3553.I78 A6 2003
2003057196

Book design by JoAnne Metsch

www.vintagebooks.com

Printed in the United States of America
10 9 8 7 6 5 4 3 2 1

CONTENTS

VINTAGE CISNEROS

HAIRS

Everybody in our family has different hair. My Papa's hair is like a broom, all up in the air. And me, my hair is lazy. It never obeys barrettes or bands. Carlos' hair is thick and straight. He doesn't need to comb it. Nenny's hair is slippery—slides out of your hand. And Kiki, who is the youngest, has hair like fur.

But my mother's hair, my mother's hair, like little rosettes, like little candy circles all curly and pretty because she pinned it in pincurls all day, sweet to put your nose into when she is holding you, holding you and you feel safe, is the warm smell of bread before you bake it, is the smell when she makes room for you on her side of the bed still warm with her skin, and you sleep near her, the rain outside falling and Papa snoring. The snoring, the rain, and Mama's hair that smells like bread.

MY NAME

In English my name means hope. In Spanish it means too many letters. It means sadness, it means waiting. It is like the number nine. A muddy color. It is the Mexican records my father plays on Sunday mornings when he is shaving, songs like sobbing.

It was my great-grandmother's name and now it is mine. She was a horse woman too, born like me in the Chinese year of the horse—which is supposed to be bad luck if you're born female—but I think this is a Chinese lie because the Chinese, like the Mexicans, don't like their women strong.

My great-grandmother. I would've liked to have known her, a wild horse of a woman, so wild she wouldn't marry. Until my great-grandfather threw a sack over her head and carried her off. Just like that, as if she were a fancy chandelier. That's the way he did it.

And the story goes she never forgave him. She looked out the window her whole life, the way so many women sit their sadness on an elbow. I wonder if she made the best with what she got or was she sorry because she couldn't be all the things she wanted to be. Esperanza. I have inherited her name, but I don't want to inherit her place by the window.

At school they say my name funny as if the syllables were made out of tin and hurt the roof of your mouth. But in Spanish my name is made out of a softer something, like silver, not quite as thick as sister's name—Magdalena—which is uglier than mine. Magdalena who at least can come home and become Nenny. But I am always Esperanza.

I would like to baptize myself under a new name, a name more like the real me, the one nobody sees. Esperanza as Lisandra or Maritza or Zeze the X. Yes. Something like Zeze the X will do.

OUR GOOD DAY

If you give me five dollars I will be your friend forever. That's what the little one tells me.

Five dollars is cheap since I don't have any friends except Cathy who is only my friend till Tuesday.

Five dollars, five dollars.

She is trying to get somebody to chip in so they can buy a bicycle from this kid named Tito. They already have ten dollars and all they need is five more.

Only five dollars, she says.

Don't talk to them, says Cathy. Can't you see they smell like a broom.

But I like them. Their clothes are crooked and old. They are wearing shiny Sunday shoes without socks. It makes their bald ankles all red, but I like them. Especially the big one who laughs with all her teeth. I like her even though she lets the little one do all the talking.

Five dollars, the little one says, only five.

Cathy is tugging my arm and I know whatever I do next will make her mad forever.

Wait a minute, I say, and run inside to get the five dollars. I have three dollars saved and I take two of Nenny's. She's not home, but I'm sure she'll be glad when she finds out we own a bike. When I get back, Cathy is gone like I knew she would be, but I don't care. I have two new friends and a bike too.

My name is Lucy, the big one says. This here is Rachel my sister.

I'm her sister, says Rachel. Who are you?

And I wish my name was Cassandra or Alexis or Maritza—anything but Esperanza—but when I tell them my name they don't laugh.

We come from Texas, Lucy says and grins. Her was born here, but me I'm Texas.

You mean *she,* I say.

No, I'm from Texas, and doesn't get it.

This bike is three ways ours, says Rachel who is thinking ahead already. Mine today, Lucy's tomorrow and yours day after.

But everybody wants to ride it today because the bike is new, so we decide to take turns *after* tomorrow. Today it belongs to all of us.

I don't tell them about Nenny just yet. It's too complicated. Especially since Rachel almost put out Lucy's eye about who was going to get to ride it first. But finally we agree to ride it together. Why not?

Because Lucy has long legs she pedals. I sit on the back seat and Rachel is skinny enough to get up on the handlebars which makes the bike all wobbly as if the wheels are spaghetti, but after a bit you get used to it.

We ride fast and faster. Past my house, sad and red and

crumbly in places, past Mr. Benny's grocery on the corner, and down the avenue which is dangerous. Laundromat junk store, drugstore, windows and cars and more cars, and around the block back to Mango.

People on the bus wave. A very fat lady crossing the street says, You sure got quite a load there.

Rachel shouts, You got quite a load there too. She is very sassy.

Down, down Mango Street we go. Rachel, Lucy, me. Our new bicycle. Laughing the crooked ride back.

THOSE WHO DON'T

Those who don't know any better come into our neighborhood scared. They think we're dangerous. They think we will attack them with shiny knives. They are stupid people who are lost and got here by mistake.

But we aren't afraid. We know the guy with the crooked eye is Davey the Baby's brother, and the tall one next to him in the straw brim, that's Rosa's Eddie V., and the big one that looks like a dumb grown man, he's Fat Boy, though he's not fat anymore nor a boy.

All brown all around, we are safe. But watch us drive into a neighborhood of another color and our knees go shakity-shake and our car windows get rolled up tight and our eyes look straight. Yeah. That is how it goes and goes.

DARIUS & THE CLOUDS

You can never have too much sky. You can fall asleep and wake up drunk on sky, and sky can keep you safe when you are sad. Here there is too much sadness and not enough sky. Butterflies too are few and so are flowers and most things that are beautiful. Still, we take what we can get and make the best of it.

Darius, who doesn't like school, who is sometimes stupid and mostly a fool, said something wise today, though most days he says nothing. Darius, who chases girls with firecrackers or a stick that touched a rat and thinks he's tough, today pointed up because the world was full of clouds, the kind like pillows.

You all see that cloud, that fat one there? Darius said, See that? Where? That one next to the one that look like popcorn. That one there. See that. That's God, Darius said. God? somebody little asked. God, he said, and made it simple.

THE FAMILY OF LITTLE FEET

There was a family. All were little. Their arms were little, and their hands were little, and their height was not tall, and their feet very small.

The grandpa slept on the living room couch and snored through his teeth. His feet were fat and doughy like thick tamales, and these he powdered and stuffed into white socks and brown leather shoes.

The grandma's feet were lovely as pink pearls and dressed in velvety high heels that made her walk with a wobble, but she wore them anyway because they were pretty.

The baby's feet had ten tiny toes, pale and see-through like a salamander's, and these he popped into his mouth whenever he was hungry.

The mother's feet, plump and polite, descended like white pigeons from the sea of pillow, across the linoleum roses, down down the wooden stairs, over the chalk hopscotch squares, 5, 6, 7, blue sky.

Do you want this? And gave us a paper bag with one pair of lemon shoes and one red and one pair of dancing shoes that used to be white but were now pale blue. Here, and we said thank you and waited until she went upstairs.

Hurray! Today we are Cinderella because our feet fit exactly, and we laugh at Rachel's one foot with a girl's gray sock and a lady's high heel. Do you like these shoes? But the truth is it is scary to look down at your foot that is no longer yours and see attached a long long leg.

Everybody wants to trade. The lemon shoes for the red shoes, the red for the pair that were once white but are now pale blue, the pale blue for the lemon, and take them off and put them back on and keep on like this a long time until we are tired.

Then Lucy screams to take our socks off and yes, it's true. We have legs. Skinny and spotted with satin scars where scabs were picked, but legs, all our own, good to look at, and long.

It's Rachel who learns to walk the best all strutted in those magic high heels. She teaches us to cross and uncross our legs, and to run like a double-dutch rope, and how to walk down to the corner so that the shoes talk back to you with every step. Lucy, Rachel, me tee-tottering like so. Down to the corner where the men can't take their eyes off us. We must be Christmas.

Mr. Benny at the corner grocery puts down his important cigar: Your mother know you got shoes like that? Who give you those?

Nobody.

Them are dangerous, he says. You girls too young to be wearing shoes like that. Take them shoes off before I call the cops, but we just run.

On the avenue a boy on a homemade bicycle calls out: Ladies, lead me to heaven.

But there is nobody around but us.

Do you like these shoes? Rachel says yes, and Lucy says yes, and yes I say, these are the best shoes. We will never go back to wearing the other kind again. Do you like these shoes?

In front of the laundromat six girls with the same fat face pretend we are invisible. They are the cousins, Lucy says, and always jealous. We just keep strutting.

Across the street in front of the tavern a bum man on the stoop.

Do you like these shoes?

Bum man says, Yes, little girl. Your little lemon shoes are so beautiful. But come closer. I can't see very well. Come closer. Please.

You are a pretty girl, bum man continues. What's your name, pretty girl?

And Rachel says Rachel, just like that.

Now you know to talk to drunks is crazy and to tell them your name is worse, but who can blame her. She is young and dizzy to hear so many sweet things in one day, even if it is a bum man's whiskey words saying them.

Rachel, you are prettier than a yellow taxicab. You know that?

But we don't like it. We got to go, Lucy says.

If I give you a dollar will you kiss me? How about a dollar. I give you a dollar, and he looks in his pocket for wrinkled money.

We have to go right now, Lucy says taking Rachel's hand because she looks like she's thinking about that dollar.

Bum man is yelling something to the air but by now we are running fast and far away, our high heel shoes taking us all the way down the avenue and around the block, past the ugly cousins, past Mr. Benny's, up Mango Street, the back way, just in case.

We are tired of being beautiful. Lucy hides the lemon shoes and the red shoes and the shoes that used to be white but are now pale blue under a powerful bushel basket on the back porch, until one Tuesday her mother, who is very clean, throws them away. But no one complains.

HIPS

I like coffee, I like tea.
I like the boys and the boys like me.
Yes, no, maybe so. Yes, no, maybe so . . .

One day you wake up and they are there. Ready and waiting like a new Buick with the keys in the ignition. Ready to take you where?

They're good for holding a baby when you're cooking, Rachel says, turning the jump rope a little quicker. She has no imagination.

You need them to dance, says Lucy.

If you don't get them you may turn into a man. Nenny says this and she believes it. She is this way because of her age.

That's right, I add before Lucy or Rachel can make fun of her. She is stupid alright, but she *is* my sister.

But most important, hips are scientific, I say repeating what Alicia already told me. It's the bones that let you know which skeleton was a man's when it was a man and which a woman's.

They bloom like roses, I continue because it's obvious I'm the only one who can speak with any authority; I have science on my side. The bones just one day open. Just like that. One day you might decide to have kids, and then where are you going to put them? Got to have room. Bones got to give.

But don't have too many or your behind will spread. That's how it is, says Rachel whose mama is as wide as a boat. And we just laugh.

What I'm saying is who here is ready? You gotta be able to know what to do with hips when you get them, I say making it up as I go. You gotta know how to walk with hips, practice you know—like if half of you wanted to go one way and the other half the other.

That's to lullaby it, Nenny says, that's to rock the baby asleep inside you. And then she begins singing *seashells, copper bells, eevy, ivy, o-ver.*

I'm about to tell her that's the dumbest thing I ever heard, but the more I think about it . . .

You gotta get the rhythm, and Lucy begins to dance. She has the idea, though she's having trouble keeping her end of the double-dutch steady.

It's gotta be just so, I say. Not too fast and not too slow. Not too fast and not too slow.

We slow the double circles down to a certain speed so Rachel who has just jumped in can practice shaking it.

I want to shake like hoochie-coochie, Lucy says. She is crazy.

I want to move like heebie-jeebie, I say picking up on the cue.

I want to be Tahiti. Or *merengue.* Or electricity.

Or *tembleque!*

Yes, *tembleque.* That's a good one.

And then it's Rachel who starts it:

Skip, skip,
snake in your hips.
Wiggle around
and break your lip.

Lucy waits a minute before her turn. She is thinking. Then she begins:

The waitress with the big fat hips
who pays the rent with taxi tips . . .
says nobody in town will kiss her on the lips
because . . .
because she looks like Christopher Columbus!
Yes, no, maybe so. Yes, no, maybe so.

She misses on maybe so. I take a little while before my turn, take a breath, and dive in:

Some are skinny like chicken lips.
Some are baggy like soggy Band-Aids
after you get out of the bathtub.
I don't care what kind I get.
Just as long as I get hips.

Everybody getting into it now except Nenny who is still humming *not a girl, not a boy, just a little baby.* She's like that.

When the two arcs open wide like jaws Nenny jumps in

across from me, the rope tick-ticking, the little gold earrings our mama gave her for her First Holy Communion bouncing. She is the color of a bar of naphtha laundry soap, she is like the little brown piece left at the end of the wash, the hard little bone, my sister. Her mouth opens. She begins:

My mother and your mother were washing clothes.
My mother punched your mother right in the nose.
What color blood came out?

Not that old song, I say. You gotta use your own song. Make it up, you know? But she doesn't get it or won't. It's hard to say which. The rope turning, turning, turning.

Engine, engine number nine,
running down Chicago line.
If the train runs off the track
do you want your money back?
Do you want your MONEY back?
Yes, no, maybe so. Yes, no, maybe so . . .

I can tell Lucy and Rachel are disgusted, but they don't say anything because she's *my* sister.

Yes, no, maybe so. Yes, no, maybe so . . .

Nenny, I say, but she doesn't hear me. She is too many light-years away. She is in a world we don't belong to anymore. Nenny. Going. Going.

Y-E-S spells yes and out you go!

ELENITA, CARDS, PALM, WATER

Elenita, witch woman, wipes the table with a rag because Ernie who is feeding the baby spilled Kool-Aid. She says: Take that crazy baby out of here and drink your Kool-Aid in the living room. Can't you see I'm busy? Ernie takes the baby into the living room where Bugs Bunny is on T.V.

Good lucky you didn't come yesterday, she says. The planets were all mixed up yesterday.

Her T.V. is color and big and all her pretty furniture made out of red fur like the teddy bears they give away in carnivals. She has them covered with plastic. I think this is on account of the baby.

Yes, it's a good thing, I say.

But we stay in the kitchen because this is where she works. The top of the refrigerator busy with holy candles, some lit, some not, red and green and blue, a plaster saint and a dusty Palm Sunday cross, and a picture of the voodoo hand taped to the wall.

Get the water, she says.

I go to the sink and pick the only clean glass there, a

beer mug that says the beer that made Milwaukee famous, and fill it up with hot water from the tap, then put the glass of water on the center of the table, the way she taught me.

Look in it, do you see anything?

But all I see are bubbles.

You see anybody's face?

Nope, just bubbles, I say.

That's okay, and she makes the sign of the cross over the water three times and then begins to cut the cards.

They're not like ordinary playing cards, these cards. They're strange, with blond men on horses and crazy baseball bats with thorns. Golden goblets, sad-looking women dressed in old-fashioned dresses, and roses that cry.

There is a good Bugs Bunny cartoon on T.V. I know, I saw it before and recognize the music and wish I could go sit on the plastic couch with Ernie and the baby, but now my fortune begins. My whole life on that kitchen table: past, present, future. Then she takes my hand and looks into my palm. Closes it. Closes her eyes too.

Do you feel it, feel the cold?

Yes, I lie, but only a little.

Good, she says, *los espíritus* are here. And begins.

This card, the one with the dark man on a dark horse, this means jealousy, and this one, sorrow. Here a pillar of bees and this a mattress of luxury. You will go to a wedding soon and did you lose an anchor of arms, yes, an anchor of arms? It's clear that's what that means.

What about a house, I say, because that's what I came for.

Ah, yes, a home in the heart. I see a home in the heart.

Is that *it?*

That's what I see, she says, then gets up because the kids are fighting. Elenita gets up to hit and then hug them. She really does love them, only sometimes they are rude.

She comes back and can tell I'm disappointed. She's a witch woman and knows many things. If you got a headache, rub a cold egg across your face. Need to forget an old romance? Take a chicken's foot, tie it with red string, spin it over your head three times, then burn it. Bad spirits keeping you awake? Sleep next to a holy candle for seven days, then on the eighth day, spit. And lots of other stuff. Only now she can tell I'm sad.

Baby, I'll look again if you want me to. And she looks again into the cards, palm, water, and says uh-huh.

A home in the heart, I was right.

Only I don't get it.

A new house, a house made of heart. I'll light a candle for you.

All this for five dollars I give her.

Thank you and good-bye and be careful of the evil eye. Come back again on a Thursday when the stars are stronger. And may the Virgin bless you. And shuts the door.

FOUR SKINNY TREES

They are the only ones who understand me. I am the only one who understands them. Four skinny trees with skinny necks and pointy elbows like mine. Four who do not belong here but are here. Four raggedy excuses planted by the city. From our room we can hear them, but Nenny just sleeps and doesn't appreciate these things.

Their strength is secret. They send ferocious roots beneath the ground. They grow up and they grow down and grab the earth between their hairy toes and bite the sky with violent teeth and never quit their anger. This is how they keep.

Let one forget his reason for being, they'd all droop like tulips in a glass, each with their arms around the other. Keep, keep, keep, trees say when I sleep. They teach.

When I am too sad and too skinny to keep keeping, when I am a tiny thing against so many bricks, then it is I look at trees. When there is nothing left to look at on this street. Four who grew despite concrete. Four who reach and do not forget to reach. Four whose only reason is to be and be.

NO SPEAK ENGLISH

Mamacita is the big mama of the man across the street, third-floor front. Rachel says her name ought to be *Mamasota,* but I think that's mean.

The man saved his money to bring her here. He saved and saved because she was alone with the baby boy in that country. He worked two jobs. He came home late and he left early. Every day.

Then one day *Mamacita* and the baby boy arrived in a yellow taxi. The taxi door opened like a waiter's arm. Out stepped a tiny pink shoe, a foot soft as a rabbit's ear, then the thick ankle, a flutter of hips, fuchsia roses and green perfume. The man had to pull her, the taxicab driver had to push. Push, pull. Push, pull. Poof!

All at once she bloomed. Huge, enormous, beautiful to look at, from the salmon-pink feather on the tip of her hat down to the little rosebuds of her toes. I couldn't take my eyes off her tiny shoes.

Up, up, up the stairs she went with the baby boy in a blue blanket, the man carrying her suitcases, her lavender hatboxes, a dozen boxes of satin high heels. Then we didn't see her.

Somebody said because she's too fat, somebody because of the three flights of stairs, but I believe she doesn't come out because she is afraid to speak English, and maybe this is so since she only knows eight words. She knows to say: *He not here* for when the landlord comes, *No speak English* if anybody else comes, and *Holy smokes.* I don't know where she learned this, but I heard her say it one time and it surprised me.

My father says when he came to this country he ate hamandeggs for three months. Breakfast, lunch and dinner. Hamandeggs. That was the only word he knew. He doesn't eat hamandeggs anymore.

Whatever her reasons, whether she is fat, or can't climb the stairs, or is afraid of English, she won't come down. She sits all day by the window and plays the Spanish radio show and sings all the homesick songs about her country in a voice that sounds like a seagull.

Home. Home. Home is a house in a photograph, a pink house, pink as hollyhocks with lots of startled light. The man paints the walls of the apartment pink, but it's not the same, you know. She still sighs for her pink house, and then I think she cries. I would.

Sometimes the man gets disgusted. He starts screaming and you can hear it all the way down the street.

Ay, she says, she is sad.

Oh, he says. Not again.

¿Cuándo, cuándo, cuándo? she asks.

¡Ay, caray! We *are* home. This *is* home. Here I am and here I stay. Speak English. Speak English. Christ!

¡Ay! Mamacita, who does not belong, every once in a while lets out a cry, hysterical, high, as if he had torn the only skinny thread that kept her alive, the only road out to that country.

And then to break her heart forever, the baby boy, who has begun to talk, starts to sing the Pepsi commercial he heard on T.V.

No speak English, she says to the child who is singing in the language that sounds like tin. No speak English, no speak English, and bubbles into tears. No, no, no, as if she can't believe her ears.

A HOUSE OF MY OWN

Not a flat. Not an apartment in back. Not a man's house. Not a daddy's. A house all my own. With my porch and my pillow, my pretty purple petunias. My books and my stories. My two shoes waiting beside the bed. Nobody to shake a stick at. Nobody's garbage to pick up after.

Only a house quiet as snow, a space for myself to go, clean as paper before the poem.

Preface from
MY WICKED WICKED WAYS

"I can live alone and I love to work." —MARY CASSATT
*"Allí está el detalle."** —CANTINFLAS

Gentlemen, ladies. If you please—these
are my wicked poems from when.
The girl grief decade. My wicked nun
years, so to speak. I sinned.

Not in the white-woman way.
Not as Simone voyeuring the pretty
slum city on a golden arm. And no,

not wicked like the captain of the bad
boy blood, that Hollywood hood-
lum who boozed and floozed it up,
hell-bent on self-destruction. Not me.
Well. Not much. Tell me,
how does a woman who.
A woman like me. Daughter of
a daddy with a hammer and blistered feet

*(Roughly translated: There's the rub.)

he'd dip into a washtub while he ate his dinner.
A woman with no birthright in the matter.

What does a woman inherit
that tells her how
to go?

My first felony—I took up with poetry.
For this penalty, the rice burned.
Mother warned I'd never wife.

Wife? A woman like me
whose choice was rolling pin or factory.
An absurd vice, this wicked wanton
writer's life.

I chucked the life
my father'd plucked for me.
Leapt into the salamander fire.
A girl who'd never roamed
beyond her father's rooster eye.
Winched the door with poetry and fled.
For good. And grieved I'd gone
when I was so alone.

In my kitchen, in the thin hour,
a calendar Cassatt chanted:
Repeat after me—
I can live alone and I love to . . .
What a crock. Each week, the ritual grief.
That decade of the knuckled knocks.

I took the crooked route and liked my badness.
Played at mistress.
Tattooed an ass.
Lapped up my happiness from a glass.
It was something, at least.

I hadn't a clue.

What does a woman
willing to invent herself
at twenty-two or twenty-nine
do? A woman with no who nor how.
And how was I to know what was unwise.

I wanted to be writer. I wanted to be happy.
What's that? At twenty. Or twenty-nine.
Love. Baby. Husband.
The works. The big palookas of life.
Wanting and not wanting.
Take your hands off me.

I left my father's house
before the brothers,
vagabonded the globe
like a rich white girl.
Got a flat.
I paid for it. I kept it clean.
Sometimes the silence frightened me.
Sometimes the silence blessed me.

It would come get me.
Late at night.
Open like a window,
hungry for my life.

I wrote when I was sad.
The flat cold.
When there was no love—
new, old—
to distract me.
No six brothers
with their Fellini racket.
No mother, father,
with their wise I told you.

I tell you,
these are the pearls
from that ten-year itch,
my jewels, my colicky kids
who fussed and kept
me up the wicked nights
when all I wanted was . . .
With nothing in the texts to tell me.

But that was then,
The who-I-was who would become the who-I-am.
These poems are from that hobbled when.

11th OF JUNE, 1992
Hydra, Greece

ABUELITO WHO

Abuelito who throws coins like rain
and asks who loves him
who is dough and feathers
who is a watch and glass of water
whose hair is made of fur
is too sad to come downstairs today
who tells me in Spanish you are my diamond
who tells me in English you are my sky
whose little eyes are string
can't come out to play
sleeps in his little room all night and day
who used to laugh like the letter k
is sick
is a doorknob tied to a sour stick
is tired shut the door
doesn't live here anymore
is hiding underneath the bed
who talks to me inside my head

is blankets and spoons and big brown shoes
who snores up and down up and down up and down again
is the rain on the roof that falls like coins
asking who loves him
who loves him who?

MY WICKED WICKED WAYS

This is my father.
See? He is young.
He looks like Errol Flynn.
He is wearing a hat
that tips over one eye,
a suit that fits him good,
and baggy pants.
He is also wearing
those awful shoes,
the two-toned ones
my mother hates.

Here is my mother.
She is not crying.
She cannot look into the lens
because the sun is bright.
The woman,
the one my father knows,

is not here.
She does not come till later.

My mother will get very mad,
Her face will turn red
and she will throw one shoe.
My father will say nothing.
After a while everyone
will forget it.
Years and years will pass.
My mother will stop mentioning it.

This is me she is carrying.
I am a baby.
She does not know
I will turn out bad.

ASS

for David

My Michelangelo!
What Bernini could compare?
Could the Borghese estate compete?
Could the Medici's famed aesthete
produce as excellent and sweet
as this famous derriere.

Did I say derriere?
Derriere too dainty.
Buttocks much too bawdy.
Cheeks so childishly petite.
Buns, impudently funny.
Rear end smacking of collision.

Ah, misnomered beauty.
Long-suffering
butt of jokes,
object of derision.
Pomegranate and apple

hath not such tempting
allure to me
as your hypnotic
anatomy.

Then
am I victim
of your spell,
bound since mine eyes
did first espy
that paradise of symmetry.

And like Pygmalion transfixed,
who sincere believed
desire could unfix
that alabaster chastity,
grieved the enchantment
of those small cruel hips—
those hard twin bones—
that house such enormous
happiness.

PEACHES—SIX IN A TIN BOWL, SARAJEVO

If peaches had arms
surely they would hold one another
in their peach sleep.

And if peaches had feet
it is sure they would
nudge one another
with their soft peachy feet.

And if peaches could
they would sleep
with their dimpled head
on the other's
each to each.

Like you and me.

And sleep and sleep.

14 DE JULIO

Today, *catorce de julio,*
a man kissed a woman in the rain.
On the corner of Independencia y Cinco de Mayo.
A man kissed a woman.

Because it is Friday.
Because no one has to go to work tomorrow.
Because, in direct opposition to Church and State,
a man kissed a woman
oblivious to the consequence of sorrow.

A man kisses a woman unashamed,
within a universe of two I'm certain.
Beside the sea of taxicabs on Cinco de Mayo.
In front of an open-air statue.
On an intersection busy with tourists and children.
Every day little miracles like this occur.

A man kisses a woman in the rain
and I am envious of that simple affirmation.
I who timidly took and timidly gave—
you who never admitted a public grace.
We of the half-dark who were unbrave.

ELEVEN

What they don't understand about birthdays and what they never tell you is that when you're eleven, you're also ten, and nine, and eight, and seven, and six, and five, and four, and three, and two, and one. And when you wake up on your eleventh birthday you expect to feel eleven, but you don't. You open your eyes and everything's just like yesterday, only it's today. And you don't feel eleven at all. You feel like you're still ten. And you are—underneath the year that makes you eleven.

Like some days you might say something stupid, and that's the part of you that's still ten. Or maybe some days you might need to sit on your mama's lap because you're scared, and that's the part of you that's five. And maybe one day when you're all grown up maybe you will need to cry like if you're three, and that's okay. That's what I tell Mama when she's sad and needs to cry. Maybe she's feeling three.

Because the way you grow old is kind of like an onion or like the rings inside a tree trunk or like my little wooden dolls that fit one inside the other, each year inside the next one. That's how being eleven years old is.

You don't feel eleven. Not right away. It takes a few days, weeks even, sometimes even months before you say Eleven when they ask you. And you don't feel smart eleven, not until you're almost twelve. That's the way it is.

Only today I wish I didn't have only eleven years rattling inside me like pennies in a tin Band-Aid box. Today I wish I was one hundred and two instead of eleven because if I was one hundred and two I'd have known what to say when Mrs. Price put the red sweater on my desk. I would've known how to tell her it wasn't mine instead of just sitting there with that look on my face and nothing coming out of my mouth.

"Whose is this?" Mrs. Price says, and she holds the red sweater up in the air for all the class to see. "Whose? It's been sitting in the coatroom for a month."

"Not mine," says everybody. "Not me."

"It has to belong to somebody," Mrs. Price keeps saying, but nobody can remember. It's an ugly sweater with red plastic buttons and a collar and sleeves all stretched out like you could use it for a jump rope. It's maybe a thousand years old and even if it belonged to me I wouldn't say so.

Maybe because I'm skinny, maybe because she doesn't like me, that stupid Sylvia Saldívar says, "I think it belongs to Rachel." An ugly sweater like that, all raggedy and old, but Mrs. Price believes her. Mrs. Price takes the sweater and puts it right on my desk, but when I open my mouth nothing comes out.

"That's not, I don't, you're not . . . Not mine," I finally say in a little voice that was maybe me when I was four.

"Of course it's yours," Mrs. Price says. "I remember you wearing it once." Because she's older and the teacher, she's right and I'm not.

Not mine, not mine, not mine, but Mrs. Price is already turning to page thirty-two, and math problem number four. I don't know why but all of a sudden I'm feeling sick inside, like the part of me that's three wants to come out of my eyes, only I squeeze them shut tight and bite down on my teeth real hard and try to remember today I am eleven, eleven. Mama is making a cake for me for tonight, and when Papa comes home everybody will sing Happy birthday, happy birthday to you.

But when the sick feeling goes away and I open my eyes, the red sweater's still sitting there like a big red mountain. I move the red sweater to the corner of my desk with my ruler. I move my pencil and books and eraser as far from it as possible. I even move my chair a little to the right. Not mine, not mine, not mine.

In my head I'm thinking how long till lunchtime, how long till I can take the red sweater and throw it over the schoolyard fence, or leave it hanging on a parking meter, or bunch it up into a little ball and toss it in the alley. Except when math period ends Mrs. Price says loud and in front of everybody, "Now, Rachel, that's enough," because she sees I've shoved the red sweater to the tippy-tip corner of my desk and it's hanging all over the edge like a waterfall, but I don't care.

"Rachel," Mrs. Price says. She says it like she's getting mad. "You put that sweater on right now and no more nonsense."

"But it's not—"

"Now!" Mrs. Price says.

This is when I wish I wasn't eleven, because all the years inside of me—ten, nine, eight, seven, six, five, four, three, two, and one—are pushing at the back of my eyes when I put one arm through one sleeve of the sweater that smells like cottage cheese, and then the other arm through the other and stand there with my arms apart like if the sweater hurts me and it does, all itchy and full of germs that aren't even mine.

That's when everything I've been holding in since this morning, since when Mrs. Price put the sweater on my desk, finally lets go, and all of a sudden I'm crying in front of everybody. I wish I was invisible but I'm not. I'm eleven and it's my birthday today and I'm crying like I'm three in front of everybody. I put my head down on the desk and bury my face in my stupid clown-sweater arms. My face all hot and spit coming out of my mouth because I can't stop the little animal noises from coming out of me, until there aren't any more tears left in my eyes, and it's just my body shaking like when you have the hiccups, and my whole head hurts like when you drink milk too fast.

But the worst part is right before the bell rings for lunch. That stupid Phyllis Lopez, who is even dumber than Sylvia Saldívar, says she remembers the red sweater is hers! I take it off right away and give it to her, only Mrs. Price pretends like everything's okay.

Today I'm eleven. There's a cake Mama's making for tonight, and when Papa comes home from work we'll eat it. There'll be candles and presents and everybody will sing Happy birthday, happy birthday to you, Rachel, only it's too late.

I'm eleven today. I'm eleven, ten, nine, eight, seven, six, five, four, three, two, and one, but I wish I was one hundred and two. I wish I was anything but eleven, because I want today to be far away already, far away like a runaway balloon, like a tiny *o* in the sky, so tiny-tiny you have to close your eyes to see it.

SALVADOR LATE OR EARLY

Salvador with eyes the color of caterpillar, Salvador of the crooked hair and crooked teeth, Salvador whose name the teacher cannot remember, is a boy who is no one's friend, runs along somewhere in that vague direction where homes are the color of bad weather, lives behind a raw wood doorway, shakes the sleepy brothers awake, ties their shoes, combs their hair with water, feeds them milk and corn flakes from a tin cup in the dim dark of the morning.

Salvador, late or early, sooner or later arrives with the string of younger brothers ready. Helps his mama, who is busy with the business of the baby. Tugs the arms of Cecilio, Arturito, makes them hurry, because today, like yesterday, Arturito has dropped the cigar box of crayons, has let go the hundred little fingers of red, green, yellow, blue, and nub of black sticks that tumble and spill over and beyond the asphalt puddles until the crossing-guard lady holds back the blur of traffic for Salvador to collect them again.

Salvador inside that wrinkled shirt, inside the throat that must clear itself and apologize each time it speaks, inside that forty-pound body of boy with its geography of scars, its history of hurt, limbs stuffed with feathers and rags, in what part of the eyes, in what part of the heart, in that cage of the chest where something throbs with both fists and knows only what Salvador knows, inside that body too small to contain the hundred balloons of happiness, the single guitar of grief, is a boy like any other disappearing out the door, beside the schoolyard gate, where he has told his brothers they must wait. Collects the hands of Cecilio and Arturito, scuttles off dodging the many schoolyard colors, the elbows and wrists criss-crossing, the several shoes running. Grows small and smaller to the eye, dissolves into the bright horizon, flutters in the air before disappearing like a memory of kites.

TEPEYAC

When the sky of Tepeyac opens its first thin stars and the dark comes down in an ink of Japanese blue above the bell towers of La Basílica de Nuestra Señora, above the plaza photographers and their souvenir backdrops of La Virgen de Guadalupe, above the balloon vendors and their balloons wearing paper hats, above the red-canopied thrones of the shoeshine stands, above the wooden booths of the women frying lunch in vats of oil, above the *tlapalería* on the corner of Misterios and Cinco de Mayo, when the photographers have toted up their tripods and big box cameras, have rolled away the wooden ponies I don't know where, when the balloon men have sold all but the ugliest balloons and herded these last few home, when the shoeshine men have grown tired of squatting on their little wooden boxes, and the women frying lunch have finished packing dishes, tablecloth, pots, in the big straw basket in which they came, then Abuelito tells the boy with dusty hair, *Arturo, we are closed,* and in crooked shoes and purple elbows Arturo pulls down with a pole the corrugated metal curtains—

first the one on Misterios, then the other on Cinco de Mayo—like an eyelid over each door, before Abuelito tells him he can go.

This is when I arrive, one shoe and then the next, over the sagging door stone, worn smooth in the middle from the huaraches of those who have come for tins of glue and to have their scissors sharpened, who have asked for candles and cans of boot polish, a half-kilo sack of nails, turpentine, blue-specked spoons, paintbrushes, photographic paper, a spool of picture wire, lamp oil, and string.

Abuelito under a bald light bulb, under a ceiling dusty with flies, puffs his cigar and counts money soft and wrinkled as old Kleenex, money earned by the plaza women serving lunch on flat tin plates, by the souvenir photographers and their canvas Recuerdo de Tepeyac backdrops, by the shoeshine men sheltered beneath their fringed and canopied kingdoms, by the blessed vendors of the holy cards, rosaries, scapulars, little plastic altars, by the good sisters who live in the convent across the street, counts and recounts in a whisper and puts the money in a paper sack we carry home.

I take Abuelito's hand, fat and dimpled in the center like a valentine, and we walk past the basilica, where each Sunday the Abuela lights the candles for the soul of Abuelito. Past the very same spot where long ago Juan Diego brought down from the *cerro* the miracle that has drawn everyone, except my Abuelito, on their knees, down the avenue one block past the bright lights of the *sastrería* of Señor Guzmán who is still at work at his sewing machine, past the candy store where I buy my milk-and-raisin gelatins, past La Providencia *tortillería* where every afternoon Luz María and I are sent for the basket of lunchtime tortillas, past the house of the widow Márquez whose husband died last winter of a tumor the size of her little white fist, past La Muñeca's mother watering her famous dahlias with a pink rubber hose and a skinny string of water, to the house on La Fortuna, number 12, that has always been our house. Green iron gates that arabesque and scroll like the initials of my name, familiar whine and clang, familiar lacework of ivy growing over and between except for one small clean square for the hand of the postman whose face I have never seen, up the twenty-two steps we count out loud together—*uno, dos, tres*—to the supper of *sopa de fideo* and *carne guisada*—*cuatro, cinco, seis*—the glass of *café con leche*—*siete, ocho, nueve*—shut the door against the mad parrot voice of the Abuela—*diez, once, doce*—fall asleep as we always do, with the television mumbling—*trece, catorce, quince*—the Abuelito snoring—*dieciséis, diecisiete, dieciocho*—the grandchild, the one who will leave soon for that borrowed country—*diecinueve, veinte, veintiuno*—the one he will not remember, the one he is least familiar with—*veintidós, veintitrés, veinticuatro*—years later when the house on La Fortuna, number 12, is sold, when the *tlapalería,* corner of Misterios and Cinco de Mayo, changes owners, when the courtyard gate of arabesques and scrolls is taken off its hinges and replaced with a corrugated sheet metal door instead, when the widow Márquez and La Muñeca's mother move away, when Abuelito falls asleep one last time—*Veinticinco, veintiséis, veintisiete*—years afterward when I return to the shop on the corner of Misterios and Cinco de Mayo, repainted and redone as a pharmacy, to the basilica that is crumbling and closed, to the plaza photographers, the balloon vendors and shoeshine thrones, the women whose faces I do not recognize serving lunch in the wooden booths, to the house on La Fortuna, number 12, smaller and darker than when we lived there, with the rooms boarded shut and rented to strangers, the street suddenly dizzy with automobiles and diesel fumes, the house fronts scuffed and the gardens frayed, the children who played kickball all grown and moved away.

Who would've guessed, after all this time, it is me who will remember when everything else is forgotten, you who took with you to your stone bed something irretrievable, without a name.

NEVER MARRY A MEXICAN

Never marry a Mexican, my ma said once and always. She said this because of my father. She said this though she was Mexican too. But she was born here in the U.S., and he was born there, and it's *not* the same, you know.

I'll *never* marry. Not any man. I've known men too intimately. I've witnessed their infidelities, and I've helped them to it. Unzipped and unhooked and agreed to clandestine maneuvers. I've been accomplice, committed premeditated crimes. I'm guilty of having caused deliberate pain to other women. I'm vindictive and cruel, and I'm capable of anything.

I admit, there was a time when all I wanted was to belong to a man. To wear that gold band on my left hand and be worn on his arm like an expensive jewel brilliant in the light of day. Not the sneaking around I did in different bars that all looked the same, red carpets with a black grillwork design, flocked wallpaper, wooden wagon-wheel light fixtures with hurricane lampshades a sick amber color like the drinking glasses you get for free at gas stations.

Dark bars, dark restaurants then. And if not—my apartment, with his toothbrush firmly planted in the toothbrush holder like a flag on the North Pole. The bed so big because he never stayed the whole night. Of course not.

Borrowed. That's how I've had my men. Just the cream skimmed off the top. Just the sweetest part of the fruit, without the bitter skin that daily living with a spouse can rend. They've come to me when they wanted the sweet meat then.

So, no. I've never married and never will. Not because I couldn't, but because I'm too romantic for marriage. Marriage has failed me, you could say. Not a man exists who hasn't disappointed me, whom I could trust to love the way I've loved. It's because I believe too much in marriage that I don't. Better to not marry than live a lie.

Mexican men, forget it. For a long time the men clearing off the tables or chopping meat behind the butcher counter or driving the bus I rode to school every day, those weren't men. Not men I considered as potential lovers. Mexican, Puerto Rican, Cuban, Chilean, Colombian, Panamanian, Salvadorean, Bolivian, Honduran, Argentine, Dominican, Venezuelan, Guatemalan, Ecuadorean, Nicaraguan, Peruvian, Costa Rican, Paraguayan, Uruguayan, I don't care. I never saw them. My mother did this to me.

I guess she did it to spare me and Ximena the pain she went through. Having married a Mexican man at seventeen. Having had to put up with all the grief a Mexican family can put on a girl because she was from *el otro lado,* the other side, and my father had married down by marrying her. If he had married a white woman from *el otro lado,* that would've been different. That would've been marrying up, even if the white girl was poor. But what could be more ridiculous than a Mexican girl who couldn't even speak Spanish, who didn't know enough to set a separate plate for each course at dinner, nor how to fold cloth napkins, nor how to set the silverware.

In my ma's house the plates were always stacked in the center of the table, the knives and forks and spoons standing in a jar, help yourself. All the dishes chipped or cracked and nothing matched. And no tablecloth, ever. And newspapers set on the table whenever my grandpa sliced watermelons, and how embarrassed she would be when her boyfriend, my father, would come over and there were newspapers all over the kitchen floor and table. And my grandpa, big hardworking Mexican man, saying Come, come and eat, and slicing a big wedge of those dark green watermelons, a big slice, he wasn't stingy with food. Never, even during the Depression. Come, come and eat, to whoever came knocking on the back door. Hobos sitting at the dinner table and the children staring and staring. Because my grandfather always made sure they never went without. Flour and rice, by the barrel and by the sack. Potatoes. Big bags of pinto beans. And watermelons, bought three or four at a time, rolled under his bed and brought out when you least expected. My grandpa had survived three wars, one Mexican, two American, and he knew what living without meant. He knew.

My father, on the other hand, did not. True, when he first came to this country he had worked shelling clams, washing dishes, planting hedges, sat on the back of the bus in Little Rock and had the bus driver shout, You—sit up here, and my father had shrugged sheepishly and said, No speak English.

But he was no economic refugee, no immigrant fleeing a war. My father ran away from home because he was afraid of facing his father after his first-year grades at the university proved he'd spent more time fooling around than studying. He left behind a house in Mexico City that was neither poor nor rich, but thought itself better than both. A boy who would get off a bus when he saw a girl he knew board if he didn't have the money to pay her fare. That was the world my father left behind.

I imagine my father in his *fanfarrón* clothes, because that's what he was, a *fanfarrón*. That's what my mother thought the moment she turned around to the voice that was asking her to dance. A big show-off, she'd say years later. Nothing but a big show-off. But she never said why she married him. My father in his shark-blue suits with the starched handkerchief in the breast pocket, his felt fedora, his tweed topcoat with the big shoulders, and heavy British wing tips with the pin-hole design on the heel and toe. Clothes that cost a lot. Expensive. That's what my father's things said. *Calidad*. Quality.

My father must've found the U.S. Mexicans very strange, so foreign from what he knew at home in Mexico City where the servant served watermelon on a plate with silverware and a cloth napkin, or mangos with their own special prongs. Not like this, eating with your legs wide open in the yard, or in the kitchen hunkered over newspapers. *Come, come and eat*. No, never like this.

How I make my living depends. Sometimes I work as a translator. Sometimes I get paid by the word and sometimes by the hour, depending on the job. I do this in the day, and at night I paint. I'd do anything in the day just so I can keep on painting.

I work as a substitute teacher, too, for the San Antonio Independent School District. And that's worse than translating those travel brochures with their tiny print, believe me. I can't stand kids. Not any age. But it pays the rent.

Any way you look at it, what I do to make a living is a form of prostitution. People say, "A painter? How nice," and want to invite me to their parties, have me decorate the lawn like an exotic orchid for hire. But do they buy art?

I'm amphibious. I'm a person who doesn't belong to any class. The rich like to have me around because they envy my creativity; they know they can't buy *that.* The poor don't mind if I live in their neighborhood because they know I'm poor like they are, even if my education and the way I dress keeps us worlds apart. I don't belong to any class. Not to the poor, whose neighborhood I share. Not to the rich, who come to my exhibitions and buy my work. Not to the middle class from which my sister Ximena and I fled.

When I was young, when I first left home and rented that apartment with my sister and her kids right after her husband left, I thought it would be glamorous to be an artist. I wanted to be like Frida or Tina. I was ready to suffer with my camera and my paint brushes in that awful apartment we rented for $150 each because it had high ceilings and those wonderful glass skylights that convinced us we had to have it. Never mind there was no sink in the bathroom, and a tub that looked like a sarcophagus, and floorboards that didn't meet, and a hallway to scare away the dead. But fourteen-foot ceilings was enough for us to write a check for the deposit right then and there. We thought it all romantic. You know the place, the one on Zarzamora on top of the barber shop with the Casasola prints of the Mexican Revolution. Neon BIRRIA TEPATITLÁN sign round the corner, two goats knocking their heads together, and all those Mexican bakeries, Las Brisas for *huevos rancheros* and *carnitas* and *barbacoa* on Sundays, and fresh fruit milk shakes, and mango *paletas,* and more signs in Spanish than in English. We thought it was great, great. The barrio looked cute in the daytime, like Sesame Street. Kids hopscotching on the sidewalk, blessed little boogers. And hardware stores that still sold ostrich-feather dusters, and whole families marching out of Our Lady of Guadalupe Church on Sundays, girls in their swirly-whirly dresses and patent-leather shoes, boys in their dress Stacys and shiny shirts.

But nights, that was nothing like what we knew up on the north side. Pistols going off like the wild, wild West, and me and Ximena and the kids huddled in one bed with the lights off listening to it all, saying, "Go to sleep, babies, it's just firecrackers." But we knew better. Ximena would say, "Clemencia, maybe we should go home." And I'd say, "Shit!" Because she knew as well as I did there was no home to go home to. Not with our mother. Not with that man she married. After Daddy died, it was like we didn't matter. Like Ma was so busy feeling sorry for herself, I don't know. I'm not like Ximena. I still haven't worked it out after all this time, even though our mother's dead now. My half brothers living in that house that should've been ours, me and Ximena's. But that's—how do you say it?—water under the damn? I can't ever get the sayings right even though I was born in this country. We didn't say shit like that in our house.

Once Daddy was gone, it was like my ma didn't exist, like if she died, too. I used to have a little finch, twisted one of its tiny red legs between the bars of the cage once, who knows how. The leg just dried up and fell off. My bird lived a long time without it, just a little red stump of a leg. He was fine, really. My mother's memory is like that, like if something already dead dried up and fell off, and I stopped missing where she used to be. Like if I never had a mother. And I'm not ashamed to say it either. When she married that white man, and he and his boys moved into my father's house, it was as if she stopped being my mother. Like I never even had one.

Ma always sick and too busy worrying about her own life, she would've sold us to the Devil if she could. "Because I married so young, *mija,*" she'd say. "Because your father, he was so much older than me, and I never had a chance to be young. Honey, try to understand . . ." Then I'd stop listening.

That man she met at work, Owen Lambert, the foreman at the photo-finishing plant, who she was seeing even while my father was sick. Even then. That's what I can't forgive.

When my father was coughing up blood and phlegm in the hospital, half his face frozen, and his tongue so fat he couldn't talk, he looked so small with all those tubes and plastic sacks dangling around him. But what I remember most is the smell, like death was already sitting on his chest. And I remember the doctor scraping the phlegm out of my father's mouth with a white washcloth, and my daddy gagging and I wanted to yell, Stop, you stop that, he's my daddy. Goddamn you. Make him live. Daddy, don't. Not yet, not yet, not yet. And how I couldn't hold myself up, I couldn't hold myself up. Like if they'd beaten me, or pulled my insides out through my nostrils, like if they'd stuffed me with cinnamon and cloves, and I just stood there dry-eyed next to Ximena and my mother, Ximena between us because I wouldn't let her stand next to me. Everyone repeating over and over the Ave Marías and Padre Nuestros. The priest sprinkling holy water, *mundo sin fin, amén.*

Drew, remember when you used to call me your Malinalli? It was a joke, a private game between us, because you looked like a Cortez with that beard of yours. My skin dark against yours. Beautiful, you said. You said I was beautiful, and when you said it, Drew, I was.

My Malinalli, Malinche, my courtesan, you said, and yanked my head back by the braid. Calling me that name in between little gulps of breath and the raw kisses you gave, laughing from that black beard of yours.

Before daybreak, you'd be gone, same as always, before I even knew it. And it was as if I'd imagined you, only the teeth marks on my belly and nipples proving me wrong.

Your skin pale, but your hair blacker than a pirate's. Malinalli, you called me, remember? *Mi doradita.* I liked when you spoke to me in my language. I could love myself and think myself worth loving.

Your son. Does he know how much I had to do with his birth? I was the one who convinced you to let him be born. Did you tell him, while his mother lay on her back laboring his birth, I lay in his mother's bed making love to you.

You're nothing without me. I created you from spit and red dust. And I can snuff you between my finger and thumb if I want to. Blow you to kingdom come. You're just a smudge of paint I chose to birth on canvas. And when I made you over, you were no longer a part of her, you were all mine. The landscape of your body taut as a drum. The heart beneath that hide thrumming and thrumming. Not an inch did I give back.

I paint and repaint you the way I see fit, even now. After all these years. Did you know that? Little fool. You think I went hobbling along with my life, whimpering and whining like some twangy country-and-western when you went back to her. But I've been waiting. Making the world look at you from my eyes. And if that's not power, what is?

Nights I light all the candles in the house, the ones to La Virgen de Guadalupe, the ones to el Niño Fidencio, Don Pedrito Jaramillo, Santo Niño de Atocha, Nuestra Señora de San Juan de los Lagos, and especially, Santa Lucía, with her beautiful eyes on a plate.

Your eyes are beautiful, you said. You said they were the darkest eyes you'd ever seen and kissed each one as if they were capable of miracles. And after you left, I wanted to scoop them out with a spoon, place them on a plate under these blue blue skies, food for the blackbirds.

The boy, your son. The one with the face of that red-headed woman who is your wife. The boy red-freckled like fish food floating on the skin of water. That boy.

I've been waiting patient as a spider all these years, since I was nineteen and he was just an idea hovering in his mother's head, and I'm the one that gave him permission and made it happen, see.

Because your father wanted to leave your mother and live with me. Your mother whining for a child, at least *that.* And he kept saying, Later, we'll see, later. But all along it was me he wanted to be with, it was me, he said.

I want to tell you this evenings when you come to see me. When you're full of talk about what kind of clothes you're going to buy, and what you used to be like when you started high school and what you're like now that you're almost finished. And how everyone knows you as a rocker, and your band, and your new red guitar that you just got because your mother gave you a choice, a guitar or a car, but you don't need a car, do you, because I drive you everywhere. You could be my son if you weren't so light-skinned.

This happened. A long time ago. Before you were born. When you were a moth inside your mother's heart, I was your father's student, yes, just like you're mine now. And your father painted and painted me, because he said, I was his *doradita,* all golden and sun-baked, and that's the kind of woman he likes best, the ones brown as river sand, yes. And he took me under his wing and in his bed, this man, this teacher, your father. I was honored that he'd done me the favor. I was that young.

All I know is I was sleeping with your father the night you were born. In the same bed where you were conceived. I was sleeping with your father and didn't give a damn about that woman, your mother. If she was a brown woman like me, I might've had a harder time living with myself, but since she's not, I don't care. I was there first, always. I've always been there, in the mirror, under his skin, in the blood, before you were born. And he's been here in my heart before I even knew him. Understand? He's always been here. Always. Dissolving like a hibiscus flower, exploding like a rope into dust. I don't care what's right anymore. I don't care about his wife. She's not *my* sister.

And it's not the last time I've slept with a man the night his wife is birthing a baby. Why do I do that, I wonder? Sleep with a man when his wife is giving life, being suckled by a thing with its eyes still shut. Why do that? It's always given me a bit of crazy joy to be able to kill those women like that, without their knowing it. To know I've had their husbands when they were anchored in blue hospital rooms, their guts yanked inside out, the baby sucking their breasts while their husband sucked mine. All this while their ass stitches were still hurting.

Once, drunk on margaritas, I telephoned your father at four in the morning, woke the bitch up. Hello, she chirped. I want to talk to Drew. Just a moment, she said in her most polite drawing-room English. Just a moment. I laughed about that for weeks. What a stupid ass to pass the phone over to the lug asleep beside her. Excuse me, honey, it's for you. When Drew mumbled hello I was laughing so hard I could hardly talk. Drew? That dumb bitch of a wife of yours, I said, and that's all I could manage. That stupid stupid stupid. No Mexican woman would react like that. Excuse me, honey. It cracked me up.

He's got the same kind of skin, the boy. All the blue veins pale and clear just like his mama. Skin like roses in December. Pretty boy. Little clone. Little cells split into you and you and you. Tell me, baby, which part of you is your mother. I try to imagine her lips, her jaw, her long long legs that wrapped themselves around this father who took me to his bed.

This happened. I'm asleep. Or pretend to be. You're watching me, Drew. I feel your weight when you sit on the corner of the bed, dressed and ready to go, but now you're just watching me sleep. Nothing. Not a word. Not a kiss. Just sitting. You're taking me in, under inspection. What do you think already?

I haven't stopped dreaming you. Did you know that? Do you think it's strange? I never tell, though. I keep it to myself like I do all the thoughts I think of you.

After all these years.

I don't want you looking at me. I don't want you taking me in while I'm asleep. I'll open my eyes and frighten you away.

There. What did I tell you? *Drew? What is it?* Nothing. I knew you'd say that.

Let's not talk. We're no good at it. With you I'm useless with words. As if somehow I had to learn to speak all over again, as if the words I needed haven't been invented yet. We're cowards. Come back to bed. At least there I feel I have you for a little. For a moment. For a catch of the breath. You let go. You ache and tug. You rip my skin.

You're almost not a man without your clothes. How do I explain it? You're so much a child in my bed. Nothing but a big boy who needs to be held. I won't let anyone hurt you. My pirate. My slender boy of a man.

After all these years.

I didn't imagine it, did I? A Ganges, an eye of the storm. For a little. When we forgot ourselves, you tugged me, I leapt inside you and split you like an apple. Opened for the other to look and not give back. Something wrenched itself loose. Your body doesn't lie. It's not silent like you.

You're nude as a pearl. You've lost your train of smoke. You're tender as rain. If I'd put you in my mouth you'd dissolve like snow.

You were ashamed to be so naked. Pulled back. But I saw you for what you are, when you opened yourself for me. When you were careless and let yourself through. I caught that catch of the breath. I'm not crazy.

When you slept, you tugged me toward you. You sought me in the dark. I didn't sleep. Every cell, every follicle, every nerve, alert. Watching you sigh and roll and turn and hug me closer to you. I didn't sleep. I was taking *you* in that time.

Your mother? Only once. Years after your father and I stopped seeing each other. At an art exhibition. A show on the photographs of Eugène Atget. Those images, I could look at them for hours. I'd taken a group of students with me.

It was your father I saw first. And in that instant I felt as if everyone in the room, all the sepia-toned photographs, my students, the men in business suits, the high-heeled women, the security guards, everyone, could see me for what I was. I had to scurry out, lead my kids to another gallery, but some things destiny has cut out for you.

He caught up with us in the coat-check area, arm in arm with a redheaded Barbie doll in a fur coat. One of those scary Dallas types, hair yanked into a ponytail, big shiny face like the women behind the cosmetic counters at Neiman's. That's what I remember. She must've been with him all along, only I swear I never saw her until that second.

You could tell from a slight hesitancy, only slight because he's too suave to hesitate, that he was nervous. Then he's walking toward me, and I didn't know what to do, just stood there dazed like those animals crossing the road at night when the headlights stun them.

And I don't know why, but all of a sudden I looked at my shoes and felt ashamed at how old they looked. And he comes up to me, my love, your father, in that way of his with that grin that makes me want to beat him, makes me want to make love to him, and he says in the most sincere voice you ever heard, "Ah, Clemencia! *This* is Megan." No introduction could've been meaner. *This* is Megan. Just like that.

I grinned like an idiot and held out my paw—"Hello, Megan"—and smiled too much the way you do when you can't stand someone. Then I got the hell out of there, chattering like a monkey all the ride back with my kids. When I got home I had to lie down with a cold washcloth on my forehead and the TV on. All I could hear throbbing under the washcloth in that deep part behind my eyes: *This* is Megan.

And that's how I fell asleep, with the TV on and every light in the house burning. When I woke up it was something like three in the morning. I shut the lights and TV and went to get some aspirin, and the cats, who'd been asleep with me on the couch, got up too and followed me into the bathroom as if they knew what's what. And then they followed me into bed, where they aren't allowed, but this time I just let them, fleas and all.

This happened, too. I swear I'm not making this up. It's all true. It was the last time I was going to be with your father. We had agreed. All for the best. Surely I could see that, couldn't I? My own good. A good sport. A young girl like me. Hadn't I understood . . . responsibilities. Besides, he could *never* marry *me.* You didn't think . . . ? *Never marry a Mexican. Never marry a Mexican* . . . No, of course not. I see. I see.

We had the house to ourselves for a few days, who knows how. You and your mother had gone somewhere. Was it Christmas? I don't remember.

I remember the leaded-glass lamp with the milk glass above the dining-room table. I made a mental inventory of everything. The Egyptian lotus design on the hinges of the doors. The narrow, dark hall where your father and I had made love once. The four-clawed tub where he had washed my hair and rinsed it with a tin bowl. This window. That counter. The bedroom with its light in the morning, incredibly soft, like the light from a polished dime.

The house was immaculate, as always, not a stray hair anywhere, not a flake of dandruff or a crumpled towel. Even the roses on the dining-room table held their breath. A kind of airless cleanliness that always made me want to sneeze.

Why was I so curious about this woman he lived with?

Every time I went to the bathroom, I found myself opening the medicine cabinet, looking at all the things that were hers. Her Estée Lauder lipsticks. Corals and pinks, of course. Her nail polishes—mauve was as brave as she could wear. Her cotton balls and blond hairpins. A pair of bone-colored sheepskin slippers, as clean as the day she'd bought them. On the door hook—a white robe with a MADE IN ITALY label, and a silky nightshirt with pearl buttons. I touched the fabrics. *Calidad.* Quality.

I don't know how to explain what I did next. While your father was busy in the kitchen, I went over to where I'd left my backpack, and took out a bag of gummy bears I'd bought. And while he was banging pots, I went around the house and left a trail of them in places I was sure *she* would find them. One in her lucite makeup organizer. One stuffed inside each bottle of nail polish. I untwisted the expensive lipsticks to their full length and smushed a bear on the top before recapping them. I even put a gummy bear in her diaphragm case in the very center of that luminescent rubber moon.

Why bother? Drew could take the blame. Or he could say it was the cleaning woman's Mexican voodoo. I knew that, too. It didn't matter. I got a strange satisfaction wandering about the house leaving them in places only she would look.

And just as Drew was shouting, "Dinner!" I saw it on the desk. One of those wooden babushka dolls Drew had brought her from his trip to Russia. I know. He'd bought one just like it for me.

I just did what I did, uncapped the doll inside a doll inside a doll, until I got to the very center, the tiniest baby inside all the others, and this I replaced with a gummy bear. And then I put the dolls back, just like I'd found them, one inside the other, inside the other. Except for the baby, which I put inside my pocket. All through dinner I kept reaching in the pocket of my jean jacket. When I touched it, it made me feel good.

On the way home, on the bridge over the *arroyo* on Guadalupe Street, I stopped the car, switched on the emergency blinkers, got out, and dropped the wooden toy into that muddy creek where winos piss and rats swim. The Barbie doll's toy stewing there in that muck. It gave me a feeling like nothing before and since.

Then I drove home and slept like the dead.

These mornings, I fix coffee for me, milk for the boy. I think of that woman, and I can't see a trace of my lover in this boy, as if she conceived him by immaculate conception.

I sleep with this boy, their son. To make the boy love me the way I love his father. To make him want me, hunger, twist in his sleep, as if he'd swallowed glass. I put him in my mouth. Here, little piece of my *corazón*. Boy with hard thighs and just a bit of down and a small hard downy ass like his father's, and that back like a valentine. Come here, *mi cariñito.* Come to *mamita*. Here's a bit of toast.

I can tell from the way he looks at me, I have him in my power. Come, sparrow. I have the patience of eternity. Come to *mamita*. My stupid little bird. I don't move. I don't startle him. I let him nibble. All, all for you. Rub his belly. Stroke him. Before I snap my teeth.

What is it inside me that makes me so crazy at 2 A.M.? I can't blame it on alcohol in my blood when there isn't any. It's something worse. Something that poisons the blood and tips me when the night swells and I feel as if the whole sky were leaning against my brain.

And if I killed someone on a night like this? And if it was *me* I killed instead, I'd be guilty of getting in the line of crossfire, innocent bystander, isn't it a shame. I'd be walking with my head full of images and my back to the guilty. Suicide? I couldn't say. I didn't see it.

Except it's not me who I want to kill. When the gravity of the planets is just right, it all tilts and upsets the visible balance. And that's when it wants to out from my eyes. That's when I get on the telephone, dangerous as a terrorist. There's nothing to do but let it come.

So. What do you think? Are you convinced now I'm as crazy as a tulip or a taxi? As vagrant as a cloud?

Sometimes the sky is so big and I feel so little at night. That's the problem with being cloud. The sky is so terribly big. Why is it worse at night, when I have such an urge to communicate and no language with which to form the words? Only colors. Pictures. And you know what I have to say isn't always pleasant.

Oh, love, there. I've gone and done it. What good is it? Good or bad, I've done what I had to do and needed to. And you've answered the phone, and startled me away like a bird. And now you're probably swearing under your breath and going back to sleep, with that wife beside you, warm, radiating her own heat, alive under the flannel and down and smelling a bit like milk and hand cream, and that smell familiar and dear to you, oh.

Human beings pass me on the street, and I want to reach out and strum them as if they were guitars. Sometimes all humanity strikes me as lovely. I just want to reach out and stroke someone, and say There, there, it's all right, honey. There, there, there.

BREAD

We were hungry. We went into a bakery on Grand Avenue and bought bread. Filled the backseat. The whole car smelled of bread. Big sourdough loaves shaped like a fat ass. Fat-ass bread, I said in Spanish, *Nalgona* bread. Fat-ass bread, he said in Italian, but I forget how he said it.

We ripped big chunks with our hands and ate. The car a pearl blue like my heart that afternoon. Smell of warm bread, bread in both fists, a tango on the tape player loud, loud, loud, because me and him, we're the only ones who can stand it like that, like if the bandoneon, violin, piano, guitar, bass, were inside us, like when he wasn't married, like before his kids, like if all the pain hadn't passed between us.

Driving down streets with buildings that remind him, he says, how charming this city is. And me remembering when I was little, a cousin's baby who died from swallowing rat poison in a building like these.

That's just how it is. And that's how we drove. With all his new city memories and all my old. Him kissing me between big bites of bread.

EYES OF ZAPATA

I put my nose to your eyelashes. The skin of the eyelids as soft as the skin of the penis, the collarbone with its fluted wings, the purple knot of the nipple, the dark, blue-black color of your sex, the thin legs and long thin feet. For a moment I don't want to think of your past nor your future. For now you are here, you are mine.

Would it be right to tell you what I do each night you sleep here? After your cognac and cigar, after I'm certain you're asleep, I examine at my leisure your black trousers with the silver buttons—fifty-six pairs on each side; I've counted them—your embroidered *sombrero* with its horsehair tassel, the lovely Dutch linen shirt, the fine braid stitching on the border of your *charro* jacket, the handsome black boots, your tooled gun belt and silver spurs. Are you my general? Or only that boy I met at the country fair in San Lázaro?

Hands too pretty for a man. Elegant hands, graceful hands, fingers smelling sweet as your Havanas. I had pretty hands once, remember? You used to say I had the prettiest hands of any woman in Cuautla. *Exquisitas* you called them, as if they were something to eat. It still makes me laugh remembering that.

Ay, but now look. Nicked and split and callused—how is it the hands get old first? The skin as coarse as the wattle of a hen. It's from the planting in the *tlacolol,* from the hard man's work I do clearing the field with the hoe and the machete, dirty work that leaves the clothes filthy, work no woman would do before the war.

But I'm not afraid of hard work or of being alone in the hills. I'm not afraid of dying or jail. I'm not afraid of the night like other women who run to the sacristy at the first call of *el gobierno*. I'm not other women.

Look at you. Snoring already? *Pobrecito*. Sleep, *papacito*. There, there. It's only me—Inés. *Duerme, mi trigueño, mi chulito, mi bebito. Ya, ya, ya*.

You say you can't sleep anywhere like you sleep here. So tired of always having to be *el gran general* Emiliano Zapata. The nervous fingers flinch, the long elegant bones shiver and twitch. Always waiting for the assassin's bullet.

Everyone is capable of becoming a traitor, and traitors must be broken, you say. A horse to be broken. A new saddle that needs breaking in. To break a spirit. Something to whip and lasso like you did in the *jaripeos* years ago.

Everything bothers you these days. Any noise, any light, even the sun. You say nothing for hours, and then when you do speak, it's an outburst, a fury. Everyone afraid of you, even your men. You hide yourself in the dark. You go days without sleep. You don't laugh anymore.

I don't need to ask; I've seen for myself. The war is not going well. I see it in your face. How it's changed over the years, Miliano. From so much watching, the face grows that way. These wrinkles new, this furrow, the jaw clenched tight. Eyes creased from learning to see in the night.

They say the widows of sailors have eyes like that, from squinting into the line where the sky and sea dissolve. It's the same with us from all this war. We're all widows. The men as well as the women, even the children. All *clinging to the tail of the horse of our* jefe *Zapata*. All of us scarred from these nine years of *aguantando*—enduring.

Yes, it's in your face. It's always been there. Since before the war. Since before I knew you. Since your birth in Anenecuilco and even before then. Something hard and tender all at once in those eyes. You knew before any of us, didn't you?

This morning the messenger arrived with the news you'd be arriving before nightfall, but I was already boiling the corn for your supper *tortillas.* I saw you riding in on the road from Villa de Ayala. Just as I saw you that day in Anenecuilco when the revolution had just begun and the government was everywhere looking for you. You were worried about the land titles, went back to dig them up from where you'd hidden them eighteen months earlier, under the altar in the village church—am I right?—reminding Chico Franco to keep them safe. *I'm bound to die,* you said, *someday. But our titles stand to be guaranteed.*

I wish I could rub the grief from you as if it were a smudge on the cheek. I want to gather you up in my arms as if you were Nicolás or Malena, run up to the hills. I know every cave and crevice, every back road and ravine, but I don't know where I could hide you from yourself. You're tired. You're sick and lonely with this war, and I don't want any of those things to ever touch you again, Miliano. It's enough for now you are here. For now. Under my roof again.

Sleep, *papacito*. It's only Inés circling above you, wide-eyed all night. The sound of my wings like the sound of a velvet cape crumpling. A warm breeze against your skin, the wide expanse of moon-white feathers as if I could touch all the walls of the house at one sweep. A rustling, then weightlessness, light scattered out the window until it's the moist night wind beneath my owl wings. Whorl of stars like the filigree earrings you gave me. Your tired horse still as tin, there, where you tied it to a *guamuchil* tree. River singing louder than ever since the time of the rains.

I scout the hillsides, the mountains. My blue shadow over the high grass and slash of *barrancas,* over the ghosts of haciendas silent under the blue night. From this height, the village looks the same as before the war. As if the roofs were still intact, the walls still whitewashed, the cobbled streets swept of rubble and weeds. Nothing blistered and burnt. Our lives smooth and whole.

Round and round the blue countryside, over the scorched fields, giddy wind barely ruffling my stiff, white feathers, above the two soldiers you left guarding our door, one asleep, the other dull from a day of hard riding. But I'm awake, I'm always awake when you are here. Nothing escapes me. No coyote in the mountains, or scorpion in the sand. Everything clear. The trail you rode here. The night jasmine with its frothy scent of sweet milk. The makeshift roof of cane leaves on our adobe house. Our youngest child of five summers asleep in her hammock—*What a little woman you are now, Malenita.* The laughing sound of the river and canals, and the high, melancholy voice of the wind in the branches of the tall pine.

I slow-circle and glide into the house, bringing the night-wind smell with me, fold myself back into my body. I haven't left you. I don't leave you, not ever. Do you know why? Because when you are gone I re-create you from memory. The scent of your skin, the mole above the broom of your mustache, how you fit in my palms. Your skin dark and rich as *piloncillo*. This face in my hands. I miss you. I miss you even now as you lie next to me.

To look at you as you sleep, the color of your skin. How in the half-light of moon you cast your own light, as if you are all made of amber, Miliano. As if you are a little lantern, and everything in the house is golden too.

You used to be *tan chistoso. Muy bonachón, muy bromista.* Joking and singing off-key when you had your little drinks. *Tres vicios tengo y los tengo muy arraigados; de ser borracho, jugador, y enamorado . . . Ay,* my life, remember? Always *muy enamorado,* no? Are you still that boy I met at the San Lázaro country fair? Am I still that girl you kissed under the little avocado tree? It seems so far away from those days, Miliano.

We drag these bodies around with us, these bodies that have nothing at all to do with you, with me, with who we really are, these bodies that give us pleasure and pain. Though I've learned how to abandon mine at will, it seems to me we never free ourselves completely until we love, when we lose ourselves inside each other. Then we see a little of what is called heaven. When we can be that close that we no longer are Inés and Emiliano, but something bigger than our lives. And we can forgive, finally.

You and I, we've never been much for talking, have we? Poor thing, you don't know how to talk. Instead of talking with your lips, you put one leg around me when we sleep, to let me know it's all right. And we fall asleep like that, with one arm or a leg or one of those long monkey feet of yours touching mine. Your foot inside the hollow of my foot.

Does it surprise you I don't let go little things like that? There are so many things I don't forget even if I would do well to.

Inés, for the love I have for you. When my father pleaded, you can't imagine how I felt. How a pain entered my heart like a current of cold water and in that current were the days to come. But I said nothing.

Well then, my father said, *God help you. You've turned out just like the* perra *that bore you.* Then he turned around and I had no father.

I never felt so alone as that night. I gathered my things in my *rebozo* and ran out into the darkness to wait for you by the *jacaranda* tree. For a moment, all my courage left me. I wanted to turn around, call out, *'apá,* beg his forgiveness, and go back to sleeping on my *petate* against the cane-rush wall, waking before dawn to prepare the corn for the day's tortillas.

Perra. That word, the way my father spat it, as if in that one word I were betraying all the love he had given me all those years, as if he were closing all the doors to his heart.

Where could I hide from my father's anger? I could put out the eyes and stop the mouths of all the saints that wagged their tongues at me, but I could not stop my heart from hearing that word—*perra.* My father, my love, who would have nothing to do with me.

You don't like me to talk about my father, do you? I know, you and he never, well . . . Remember that thick scar across his left eyebrow? Kicked by a mule when he was a boy. Yes, that's how it happened. Tía Chucha said it was the reason he sometimes acted like a mule—but you're as stubborn as he was, aren't you, and no mule kicked you.

It's true, he never liked you. Since the days you started buying and selling livestock all through the *rancheritos*. By the time you were working the stables in Mexico City there was no mentioning your name. Because you'd never slept under a thatch roof, he said. Because you were a *charro,* and didn't wear the cotton whites of the *campesino*. Then he'd mutter, loud enough for me to hear, *That one doesn't know what it is to smell his own shit.*

I always thought you and he made such perfect enemies because you were so much alike. Except, unlike you, he was useless as a soldier. I never told you how the government forced him to enlist. Up in Guanajuato is where they sent him when you were busy with the Carrancistas, and Pancho Villa's boys were giving everyone a rough time up north. My father, who'd never been farther than Amecameca, gray-haired and broken as he was, they took him. It was during the time the dead were piled up on the street corners like stones, when it wasn't safe for anyone, man or woman, to go out into the streets.

There was nothing to eat, Tía Chucha sick with the fever, and me taking care of us all. My father said better he should go to his brother Fulgencio's in Tenexcapán and see if they had corn there. *Take Malenita,* I said. *With a child they won't bother you.*

And so my father went out toward Tenexcapán dragging

Malenita by the hand. But when night began to fall and they hadn't come back, well, imagine. It was the widow Elpidia who knocked on our door with Malenita howling and with the story they'd taken the men to the railroad station. *South to the work camps, or north to fight?* Tía Chucha asked. *If God wishes,* I said, *he'll be safe.*

That night Tía Chucha and I dreamt this dream. My father and my Tío Fulgencio standing against the back wall of the rice mill. *Who lives?* But they don't answer, afraid to give the wrong *viva. Shoot them; discuss politics later.*

At the moment the soldiers are about to fire, an officer, an acquaintance of my father's from before the war, rides by and orders them set free.

Then they took my father and my Tío Fulgencio to the train station, shuttled them into box cars with others, and didn't let them go until they reached Guanajuato where they were each given guns and orders to shoot at the Villistas.

With the fright of the firing squad and all, my father was never the same. In Guanajuato, he had to be sent to the military hospital, where he suffered a collapsed lung. They removed three of his ribs to cure him, and when he was finally well enough to travel, they sent him back to us.

All through the dry season my father lived on like that, with a hole in the back of his chest from which he breathed. Those days I had to swab him with a sticky pitch pine and wrap him each morning in clean bandages. The opening oozed a spittle like the juice of the prickly pear, sticky and clear and with a smell both sweet and terrible like magnolia flowers rotting on the branch.

We did the best we could to nurse him, my Tía Chucha

and I. Then one morning a *chachalaca* flew inside the house and battered against the ceiling. It took both of us with blankets and the broom to get it out. We didn't say anything but we thought about it for a long time.

Before the next new moon, I had a dream I was in church praying a rosary. But what I held between my hands wasn't my rosary with the glass beads, but one of human teeth. I let it drop, and the teeth bounced across the flagstones like pearls from a necklace. The dream and the bird were sign enough.

When my father called my mother's name one last time and died, the syllables came out sucked and coughed from that other mouth, like a drowned man's, and he expired finally in one last breath from that opening that killed him.

We buried him like that, with his three missing ribs wrapped in a handkerchief my mother had embroidered with his initials and with the hoofmark of the mule under his left eyebrow.

For eight days people arrived to pray the rosary. All the priests had long since fled, we had to pay a *rezandero* to say the last rites. Tía Chucha laid the cross of lime and sand, and set out flowers and a votive lamp, and on the ninth day, my *tía* raised the cross and called out my father's name—Remigio Alfaro—and my father's spirit flew away and left us.

But suppose he won't give us his permission.

That old goat, we'll be dead by the time he gives his permission. Better we just run off. He can't be angry forever.

Not even on his deathbed did he forgive you. I suppose you've never forgiven him either for calling in the authorities. I'm sure he only meant for them to scare you a little, to remind you of your obligations to me since I was expecting your child. Who could imagine they would force you to join the cavalry.

I can't make apologies on my father's behalf, but, well, what were we to think, Miliano? Those months you were gone, hiding out in Puebla because of the protest signatures, the political organizing, the work in the village defense. Me as big as a boat, Nicolás waiting to be born at any moment, and you nowhere to be found, and no money sent, and not a word. I was so young, I didn't know what else to do but abandon our house of stone and adobe and go back to my father's. Was I wrong to do that? You tell me.

I could endure my father's anger, but I was afraid for the child. I placed my hand on my belly and whispered—Child, be born when the moon is tender; even a tree must be pruned under the full moon so it will grow strong. And at the next full moon, I gave light, Tía Chucha holding up our handsome, strong-lunged boy.

Two planting seasons came and went, and we were preparing for the third when you came back from the cavalry and met your son for the first time. I thought you'd forgotten all about politics, and we could go on with our lives. But by the end of the year you were already behind the campaign to elect Patricio Leyva governor, as if all the troubles with the government, with my father, had meant nothing.

You gave me a pair of gold earrings as a wedding gift, remember? *I never said I'd marry you, Inés. Never.* Two filigree hoops with tiny flowers and fringe. I buried them when the government came, and went back for them later.

But even these I had to sell when there was nothing to eat but boiled corn silk. They were the last things I sold.

Never. It made me feel a little crazy when you hurled that at me. That word with all its force.

But, Miliano, I thought . . .

You were foolish to have thought then.

That was years ago. We're all guilty of saying things we don't mean. *I never said . . .* I know. You don't want to hear it.

What am I to you now, Miliano? When you leave me? When you hesitate? Hover? The last time you gave a sigh that would fit into a spoon. What did you mean by that?

If I complain about these woman concerns of mine, I know you'll tell me—Inés, these aren't times for that—wait until later. But, Miliano, I'm tired of being told to wait.

Ay, you don't understand. Even if you had the words, you could never tell me. You don't know your own heart, men. Even when you are speaking with it in your hand.

I have my livestock, a little money my father left me. I'll set up a house for us in Cuautla of stone and adobe. We can live together, and later we'll see.

Nicolás is crazy about his two cows, La Fortuna *y* La Paloma. Because he's a man now, you said, when you gave him his birthday present. When you were thirteen, you were already buying and reselling animals throughout the ranches. To see if a beast is a good worker, you must tickle it on the back, no? If it can't bother itself to move, well then, it's lazy and won't be of any use. See, I've learned that much from you.

Remember the horse you found in Cuernavaca? Someone had hidden it in an upstairs bedroom, wild and spirited from being penned so long. She had poked her head from between the gold fringe of velvet drapery just as you rode by, just at that moment. A beauty like that making her appearance from a balcony like a woman waiting for her serenade. You laughed and joked about that and named her La Coquetona, remember? La Coquetona, yes.

When I met you at the country fair in San Lázaro, everyone knew you were the best man with horses in the state of Morelos. All the hacienda owners wanted you to work for them. Even as far as Mexico City. A *charro* among *charros*. The livestock, the horses bought and sold. Planting a bit when things were slow. Your brother Eufemio borrowing time and time again because he'd squandered every *peso* of his inheritance, but you've always prided yourself in being independent, no? You once confessed one of the happiest days of your life was the watermelon harvest that produced the 600 *pesos*.

And *my* happiest memory? The night I came to live with you, of course. I remember how your skin smelled sweet as the rind of a watermelon, like the fields after it has rained. I wanted my life to begin there, at that moment when I balanced that thin boy's body of yours on mine, as if you were made of balsa, as if you were boat and I river. The days to come, I thought, erasing the bitter sting of my father's good-bye.

There's been too much suffering, too much of our hearts hardening and drying like corpses. We've survived, eaten grass and corn cobs and rotten vegetables. And the epidemics have been as dangerous as the *federales,* the deserters, the bandits. Nine years.

In Cuautla it stank from so many dead. Nicolás would go out to play with the bullet shells he'd collected, or to watch the dead being buried in trenches. Once five federal corpses were piled up in the *zócalo*. We went through their pockets for money, jewelry, anything we could sell. When they burned the bodies, the fat ran off them in streams, and they jumped and wiggled as if they were trying to sit up. Nicolás had terrible dreams after that. I was too ashamed to tell him I did, too.

At first we couldn't bear to look at the bodies hanging in the trees. But after many months, you get used to them, curling and drying into leather in the sun day after day, dangling like earrings, so that they no longer terrify, they no longer mean anything. Perhaps that is worst of all.

Your sister tells me Nicolás takes after you these days, nervous and quick with words, like a sudden dust storm or shower of sparks. When you were away with the Seventh Cavalry, Tía Chucha and I would put smoke in Nicolás's mouth, so he would learn to talk early. All the other babies his age babbling like monkeys, but Nicolás always silent, always following us with those eyes all your kin have. Those are not Alfaro eyes, I remember my father saying.

The year you came back from the cavalry, you sent for us, me and the boy, and we lived in the house of stone and adobe. From your silences, I understood I was not to question our marriage. It was what it was. Nothing more. Wondering where you were the weeks I didn't see you, and why it was you arrived only for a few slender nights, always after nightfall and leaving before dawn. Our lives ran along as they had before. What good is it to have a husband and not have him? I thought.

When you began involving yourself with the Patricio Leyva campaign, we didn't see you for months at a time. Sometimes the boy and I would return to my father's house where I felt less alone. *Just for a few nights,* I said, unrolling a *petate* in my old corner against the cane-rush wall in the kitchen. *Until my husband returns*. But a few nights grew into weeks, and the weeks into months, until I spent more time under my father's thatch roof than in our house with the roof of tiles.

That's how the weeks and months passed. Your election to the town council. Your work defending the land titles. Then the parceling of the land when your name began to run all along the villages, up and down the Cuautla River. Zapata this and Zapata that. I couldn't go anywhere without hearing it. And each time, a kind of fear entered my heart like a cloud crossing the sun.

I spent the days chewing on this poison as I was grinding the corn, pretending to ignore what the other women washing at the river said. That you had several *pastimes*. That there was a certain María Josefa in Villa de Ayala. Then they would just laugh. It was worse for me those nights you did arrive and lay asleep next to me. I lay awake watching and watching you.

In the day, I could support the grief, wake up before dawn to prepare the day's *tortillas,* busy myself with the chores, the turkey hens, the planting and collecting of herbs. The boy already wearing his first pair of trousers and getting into all kinds of trouble when he wasn't being watched. There was enough to distract me in the day. But at night, you can't imagine.

Tía Chucha made me drink heart-flower tea—*yoloxo-*

chitl, flower from the magnolia tree—petals soft and seamless as a tongue. *Yoloxochitl, flor de corazón,* with its breath of vanilla and honey. She prepared a tonic with the dried blossoms and applied a salve, mixed with the white of an egg, to the tender skin above my heart.

It was the season of rain. *Plum . . . plum plum.* All night I listened to that broken string of pearls, bead upon bead upon bead rolling across the waxy leaves of my heart.

I lived with that heartsickness inside me, Miliano, as if the days to come did not exist. And when it seemed the grief would not let me go, I wrapped one of your handkerchiefs around a dried hummingbird, went to the river, whispered, *Virgencita, ayúdame,* kissed it, then tossed the bundle into the waters where it disappeared for a moment before floating downstream in a dizzy swirl of foam.

That night, my heart circled and fluttered against my chest, and something beneath my eyelids palpitated so furiously, it wouldn't let me sleep. When I felt myself whirling against the beams of the house, I opened my eyes. I could see perfectly in the darkness. Beneath me—all of us asleep. Myself, there, in my *petate* against the kitchen wall, the boy asleep beside me. My father and my Tía Chucha sleeping in their corner of the house. Then I felt the room circle once, twice, until I found myself under the stars flying above the little avocado tree, above the house and the corral.

I passed the night in a delirious circle of sadness, of joy, reeling round and round above our roof of dried sugarcane leaves, the world as clear as if the noon sun shone. And when dawn arrived I flew back to my body that waited patiently for me where I'd left it, on the *petate* beside our Nicolás.

Each evening I flew a wider circle. And in the day, I

withdrew further and further into myself, living only for those night flights. My father whispered to my Tía Chucha, *Ojos que no ven, corazón que no siente.* But my eyes did see and my heart suffered.

One night over *milpas* and beyond the *tlacolol,* over *barrancas* and thorny scrub forests, past the thatch roofs of the *jacales* and the stream where the women do the wash, beyond bright bougainvillea, high above canyons and across fields of rice and corn, I flew. The gawky stalks of banana trees swayed beneath me. I saw rivers of cold water and a river of water so bitter they say it flows from the sea. I didn't stop until I reached a grove of high laurels rustling in the center of a town square where all the whitewashed houses shone blue as abalone under the full moon. And I remember my wings were blue and soundless as the wings of a *tecolote.*

And when I alighted on the branch of a tamarind tree outside a window, I saw you asleep next to that woman from Villa de Ayala, that woman who is your wife sleeping beside you. And her skin shone blue in the moonlight and you were blue as well.

She wasn't at all like I'd imagined. I came up close and studied her hair. Nothing but an ordinary woman with her ordinary woman smell. She opened her mouth and gave a moan. And you pulled her close to you, Miliano. Then I felt a terrible grief inside me. The two of you asleep like that, your leg warm against hers, your foot inside the hollow of her foot.

They say I am the one who caused her children to die. From jealousy, from envy. What do you say? Her boy and girl both dead before they stopped sucking teat. She won't bear you any more children. But my boy, my girl are alive.

When a customer walks away after you've named your price, and then he comes back, that's when you raise your price. When you know you have what he wants. Something I learned from your horse-trading years.

You married her, that woman from Villa de Ayala, true. But see, you came back to me. You always come back. In between and beyond the others. That's my magic. You come back to me.

You visited me again Thursday last. I yanked you from the bed of that other one. I dreamt you, and when I awoke I was sure your spirit had just fluttered from the room. I have yanked you from your sleep before into the dream I was dreaming. Twisted you like a spiral of hair around a finger. Love, you arrived with your heart full of birds. And when you would not do my bidding and come when I commanded, I turned into the soul of a *tecolote* and kept vigil in the branches of a purple *jacaranda* outside your door to make sure no one would do my Miliano harm while he slept.

You sent a letter by messenger how many months afterward? On paper thin and crinkled as if it had been made with tears.

I burned copal in a clay bowl. Inhaled the smoke. Said a prayer in *mexicano* to the old gods, an Ave María in Spanish to La Virgen, and gave thanks. You were on your way home to us. The house of stone and *adobe* aired and swept clean, the night sweet with the scent of candles that had been burning continually since I saw you in the dream. Sometime after Nicolás had fallen asleep, the hoofbeats.

A silence between us like a language. When I held you, you trembled, a tree in rain. *Ay,* Miliano, I remember that, and it helps the days pass without bitterness.

What did you tell her about me? *That was before I knew you, Josefa. That chapter of my life with Inés Alfaro is finished.* But I'm a story that never ends. Pull one string and the whole cloth unravels.

Just before you came for Nicolás, he fell ill with the symptoms of the jealousy sickness, big boy that he was. But it was true, I was with child again. Malena was born without making a sound, because she remembered how she had been conceived—nights tangled around each other like smoke.

You and Villa were marching triumphantly down the streets of Mexico City, your hat filled with flowers the pretty girls tossed at you. The brim sagging under the weight like a basket.

I named our daughter after my mother. María Elena. Against my father's wishes.

You have your *pastimes*. That's how it's said, no? Your many *pastimes*. I know you take to your bed women half my age. Women the age of our Nicolás. You've left many mothers crying, as they say.

They say you have three women in Jojutla, all under one roof. And that your women treat each other with *a most extraordinary harmony, sisters in a cause who believe in the greater good of the revolution*. I say they can all go to hell, those newspaper journalists and the mothers who bore them. Did they ever ask me?

These stupid country girls, how can they resist you? The magnificent Zapata in his elegant *charro* costume, riding a splendid horse. Your wide *sombrero* a halo around your face. You're not a man for them; you're a legend, a myth, a god. But you are as well my husband. Albeit only sometimes.

How can a woman be happy in love? To love like this, to love as strong as we hate. That is how we are, the women of my family. We never forget a wrong. We know how to love and we know how to hate.

I've seen your other children in the dreams. María Luisa from that Gregoria Zúñiga in Quilamula after her twin sister Luz died on you childless. Diego born in Tlatizapán of that woman who calls herself *Missus* Jorge Piñeiro. Ana María in Cuautla from that she-goat Petra Torres. Mateo, son of that nobody, Jesusa Pérez of Temilpa. All your children born with those eyes of Zapata.

I know what I know. How you sleep cradled in my arms, how you love me with a pleasure close to sobbing, how I still the trembling in your chest and hold you, hold you, until those eyes look into mine.

Your eyes. *Ay!* Your eyes. Eyes with teeth. Terrible as obsidian. The days to come in those eyes, *el porvenir,* the days gone by. And beneath that fierceness, something ancient and tender as rain.

Miliano, Milianito. And I sing you that song I sang Nicolás and Malenita when they were little and would not sleep.

———

Seasons of war, a little half-peace now and then, and then war and war again. Running up to the hills when the *federales* come, coming back down when they've gone.

Before the war, it was the *caciques* who were after the young girls and the married women. They had their hands on everything it seems—the land, law, women. Remember when they found that *desgraciado* Policarpo Cisneros in the arms of the Quintero girl? *¡Virgen purísima!* She was only a little thing of twelve years. And he, what? At least eighty, I imagine.

Desgraciados. All members of one army against us, no? The *federales,* the *caciques,* one as bad as the other, stealing our hens, stealing the women at night. What long sharp howls the women would let go when they carried them off. The next morning the women would be back, and we would say *Buenos días,* as if nothing had happened.

Since the war began, we've gotten used to sleeping in the corral. Or in the hills, in trees, in caves with the spiders and scorpions. We hide ourselves as best we can when the *federales* arrive, behind rocks or in *barrancas,* or in the pine and tall grass when there is nothing else to hide behind. Sometimes I build a shelter for us with cane branches in the mountains. Sometimes the people of the cold lands give us boiled water sweetened with cane sugar, and we stay until we can gather a little strength, until the sun has warmed our bones and it is safe to come back down.

Before the war, when Tía Chucha was alive, we passed the days selling at all the town markets—chickens, turkey hens, cloth, coffee, the herbs we collected in the hills or grew in the garden. That's how our weeks and months came and went.

I sold bread and candles. I planted corn and beans back then and harvested coffee at times too. I've sold all kinds of things. I even know how to buy and resell animals. And now I know how to work the *tlacolol,* which is the worst of all—your hands and feet split and swollen from the machete and hoe.

Sometimes I find sweet potatoes in the abandoned fields, or squash, or corn. And this we eat raw, too tired, too hungry to cook anything. We've eaten like the birds, what we could pluck from the trees—guava, mango, tamarind, almond when in season. We've gone without corn for the *tortillas,* made do when there were no kernels to be had, eaten the cobs as well as the flower.

My *metate,* my good shawl, my fancy *huipil,* my filigree earrings, anything I could sell, I've sold. The corn sells for one peso and a half a *cuartillo* when one can find a handful. I soak and boil and grind it without even letting it cool, a few tortillas to feed Malenita, who is always hungry, and if there is anything left, I feed myself.

Tía Chucha caught the sickness of the wind in the hot country. I used all her remedies and my own, *guacamaya* feathers, eggs, cocoa beans, chamomile oil, rosemary, but there was no help for her. I thought I would finish myself crying, all my mother's people gone from me, but there was the girl to think about. Nothing to do but go on, *aguantar,* until I could let go that grief. *Ay,* how terrible those times.

I go on surviving, hiding, searching if only for Malenita's sake. Our little plantings, that's how we get along. The government run off with the *maíz,* the chickens, my prize turkey hens and rabbits. Everyone has had his turn to do us harm.

Now I'm going to tell you about when they burned the house, the one you bought for us. I was sick with the fever. Headache and a terrible pain in the back of my calves. Fleas, babies crying, gunshots in the distance, someone crying out *el gobierno,* a gallop of horses in my head, and the shouting of those going off to join troops and of those staying. I could barely manage to drag myself up the hills. Malenita was suffering one of her *corajes* and refused to walk, sucking the collar of her blouse and crying. I had to carry her on my back with her little feet kicking me all the way until I gave her half of a hard *tortilla* to eat and she forgot about her anger and fell asleep. By the time the sun was strong and we were far away enough to feel safe, I was weak. I slept without dreaming, holding Malenita's cool body against my burning. When I woke the world was filled with stars, and the stars carried me back to the village and showed me.

It was like this. The village did not look like our village. The trees, the mountains against the sky, the land, yes, that was still as we remembered it, but the village was no longer a village. Everything pocked and in ruins. Our house with its roof tiles gone. The walls blistered and black. Pots, pans, jugs, dishes axed into shards, our shawls and blankets torn and trampled. The seed we had left, what we'd saved and stored that year, scattered, the birds enjoying it.

Hens, cows, pigs, goats, rabbits, all slaughtered. Not even the dogs were spared and were strung from the trees. The Carrancistas destroyed everything, because, as they say, *Even the stones here are Zapatistas.* And what was not destroyed was carried off by their women, who descended behind them like a plague of vultures to pick us clean.

It's *her* fault, the villagers said when they returned. *Nagual. Bruja.* Then I understood how alone I was.

Miliano, what I'm about to say to you now, only to you do I tell it, to no one else have I confessed it. It's necessary I say it; I won't rest until I undo it from my heart.

They say when I was a child I caused a hailstorm that ruined the new corn. When I was so young I don't even remember. In Tetelcingo that's what they say.

That's why the years the harvest was bad and the times especially hard, they wanted to burn me with green wood. It was my mother they killed instead, but not with green wood. When they delivered her to our door, I cried until I finished myself crying. I was sick, sick, for several days, and they say I vomited worms, but I don't remember that. Only the terrible dreams I suffered during the fever.

My Tía Chucha cured me with branches from the pepper tree and with the broom. And for a long time afterward, my legs felt as if they were stuffed with rags, and I kept seeing little purple stars winking and whirling just out of reach.

It wasn't until I was well enough to go outside again that I noticed the crosses of pressed *pericón* flowers on all the village doorways and in the *milpa* too. From then on the villagers avoided me, as if they meant to punish me by not talking, just as they'd punished my mother with those words that thumped and thudded like the hail that killed the corn.

That's why we had to move the seven kilometers from Tetelcingo to Cuautla, as if we were from that village and not the other, and that's how it was we came to live with my Tía Chucha, little by little taking my mother's place as my teacher, and later as my father's wife.

My Tía Chucha, she was the one who taught me to use my sight, just as her mother had taught her. The women in my family, we've always had the power to see with more than our eyes. My mother, my Tía Chucha, me. Our Malenita as well.

It's only now when they murmur *bruja, nagual,* behind my back, just as they hurled those words at my mother, that I realize how alike my mother and I are. How words can hold their own magic. How a word can charm, and how a word can kill. This I've understood.

Mujeriego. I dislike the word. Why not *hombreriega?* Why not? The word loses its luster. *Hombreriega*. Is that what I am? My mother? But in the mouth of men, the word is flint-edged and heavy, makes a drum of the body, something to maim and bruise, and sometimes kill.

What is it I am to you? Sometime wife? Lover? Whore? Which? To be one is not so terrible as being all.

I've needed to hear it from you. To verify what I've always thought I knew. You'll say I've grown crazy from living on dried grass and corn silk. But I swear I've never seen more clearly than these days.

Ay, Miliano, don't you see? The wars begin here, in our hearts and in our beds. You have a daughter. How do you want her treated? Like you treated me?

All I've wanted was words, that magic to soothe me a little, what you could not give me.

The months I disappeared, I don't think you understood my reasons. I assumed I made no difference to you. Only Nicolás mattered. And that's when you took him from me.

When Nicolás lost his last milk tooth, you sent for him, left him in your sister's care. He's lived like deer in the mountains, sometimes following you, sometimes meeting you ahead of your campaigns, always within reach. I know. I let him go. I agreed, yes, because a boy should be with his father, I said. But the truth is I wanted a part of me always hovering near you. How hard it must be for you to keep letting Nicolás go. And yet, he is always yours. Always.

When the *federales* captured Nicolás and took him to Tepaltzingo, you arrived with him asleep in your arms after your brother and Chico Franco rescued him. If anything happens to this child, you said, if anything . . . and started to cry. I didn't say anything, Miliano, but you can't imagine how in that instant, I wanted to be small and fit inside your heart, I wanted to belong to you like the boy, and know you loved me.

If I am a witch, then so be it, I said. And I took to eating black things—*huitlacoche* the corn mushroom, coffee, dark *chiles,* the bruised part of fruit, the darkest, blackest things to make me hard and strong.

You rarely talk. Your voice, Miliano, thin and light as a woman's, almost delicate. Your way of talking is sudden, quick, like water leaping. And yet I know what that voice of yours is capable of.

I remember after the massacre of Tlatizapán, 286 men and women and children slaughtered by the Carrancistas. Your thin figure, haggard and drawn, your face small and dark under your wide *sombrero.* I remember even your horse looked half-starved and wild that dusty, hot June day.

It was as if misery laughed at us. Even the sky was sad, the light leaden and dull, the air sticky and everything covered with flies. Women filled the streets searching among the corpses for their dead.

Everyone was tired, exhausted from running from the Carrancistas. The government had chased us almost as far as Jojutla. But you spoke in *mexicano,* you spoke to us in our language, with your heart in your hand, Miliano, which is why we listened to you. The people were tired, but they listened. Tired of surviving, of living, of enduring. Many were deserting and going back to their villages. *If you don't want to fight anymore,* you said, *we'll all go to the devil. What do you mean you are tired? When you elected me, I said I would represent you if you backed me. But now you must back me, I've kept my word. You wanted a man who wore pants, and I've been that man. And now, if you don't mean to fight, well then, there's nothing I can do.*

We were filthy, exhausted, hungry, but we followed you.

Under the little avocado tree behind my father's house is where you first kissed me. A crooked kiss, all wrong, on the side of the mouth. *You belong to me now,* you said, and I did.

The way you rode in the morning of the San Lázaro fair on a pretty horse as dark as your eyes. The sky was sorrel-colored, remember? Everything swelled and smelled of rain. A cool shadow fell across the village. You were dressed all in black as is your custom. A graceful, elegant man, thin and tall.

You wore a short black linen *charro* jacket, black trousers of cashmere adorned with silver buttons, and a lavender shirt knotted at the collar with a blue silk neckerchief. Your *sombrero* had a horsehair braid and tassel and a border of carnations embroidered along the wide brim in gold and silver threads. You wore the *sombrero* set forward—not at the back of the head as others do—so it would shade those eyes of yours, those eyes that watched and waited. Even then I knew it was an animal to match mine.

Suppose my father won't let me?

We'll run off, he can't be angry for always.

Wait until the end of the harvest.

You pulled me toward you under the little avocado tree and kissed me. A kiss tasting of warm beer and whiskers. *You belong to me now.*

It was during the plum season we met. I saw you at the country fair at San Lázaro. I wore my braids up away from the neck with bright ribbons. My hair freshly washed and combed with oil prepared with the ground bone of the *mamey.* And the neckline of my *huipil,* a white one, I remember, showed off my neck and collarbones.

You were riding a fine horse, silver-saddled with a fringe of red and black silk tassels, and your hands, beautiful hands, long and sensitive, rested lightly on the reins. I was afraid of you at first, but I didn't show it. How pretty you made your horse prance.

You circled when I tried to cross the *zócalo,* I remember. I pretended not to see you until you rode your horse in my path, and I tried to dodge one way, then the other, like a calf in a *jaripeo*. I could hear the laughter of your friends from under the shadows of the arcades. And when it was clear there was no avoiding you, I looked up at you and said, *With your permission*. You did not insist, you touched the brim of your hat, and let me go, and I heard your friend Francisco Franco, the one I would later know as Chico, say, *Small, but bigger than you, Miliano*.

So is it yes? I didn't know what to say, I was still so little, just laughed, and you kissed me like that, on my teeth.

Yes? and pressed me against the avocado tree. *No, is it?* And I said yes, then I said no, and yes, your kisses arriving in between.

Love? We don't say that word. For you it has to do with stroking with your eyes what catches your fancy, then lassoing and harnessing and corraling. Yanking home what is easy to take.

But not for me. Not from the start. You were handsome, yes, but I didn't like handsome men, thinking they could have whomever they wanted. I wanted to be, then, the one you could not have. I didn't lower my eyes like the other girls when I felt you looking at me.

I'll set up a house for us. We can live together, and later we'll see.

But suppose one day you leave me.

Never.

Wait at least until the end of the harvest.

I remember how your skin burned to the touch. How you smelled of lemongrass and smoke. I balanced that thin boy's body of yours on mine.

Something undid itself—gently, like a braid of hair unraveling. And I said, *Ay, mi chulito, mi chulito, mi chulito,* over and over.

Mornings and nights I think your scent is still in the blankets, wake remembering you are tangled somewhere between the sleeping and the waking. The scent of your skin, the mole above the broom of your thick mustache, how you fit in my hands.

Would it be right to tell you, each night you sleep here, after your cognac and cigar, when I'm certain you are finally sleeping, I sniff your skin. Your fingers sweet with the scent of tobacco. The fluted collarbones, the purple knot of the nipple, the deep, plum color of your sex, the thin legs and long, thin feet.

I examine at my leisure your black trousers with the silver buttons, the lovely shirt, the embroidered *sombrero,* the fine braid stitching on the border of your *charro* jacket, admire the workmanship, the spurs, leggings, the handsome black boots.

And when you are gone, I re-create you from memory. Rub warmth into your fingertips. Take that dimpled chin of yours between my teeth. All the parts are there except your belly. I want to rub my face in its color, say no, no, no. *Ay.* Feel its warmth from my left cheek to the right. Run my tongue from the hollow in your throat, between the smooth stones of your chest, across the trail of down below the navel, lose myself in the dark scent of your sex. To look at you as you sleep, the color of your skin. How in the half-light of moon you cast your own light, as if you are a man made of amber.

Are you my general? Or only my Milianito? I think, I don't know what you say, you don't belong to me nor to that woman from Villa de Ayala. You don't belong to anyone, no? Except the land. *La madre tierra que nos mantiene y cuida.* Every one of us.

I rise high and higher, the house shutting itself like an eye. I fly farther than I've ever flown before, farther than the clouds, farther than our Lord Sun, husband of the moon. Till all at once I look beneath me and see our lives, clear and still, far away and near.

And I see our future and our past, Miliano, one single thread already lived and nothing to be done about it. And I see the face of the man who will betray you. The place and the hour. The gift of a horse the color of gold dust. A breakfast of warm beer swirling in your belly. The hacienda gates opening. The pretty bugles doing the honors. *Tirri-LEE tirREE.* Bullets like a sudden shower of stones. And in that instant, a feeling of relief almost. And loneliness, just like that other loneliness of being born.

And I see my clean *huipil* and my silk Sunday shawl. My rosary placed between my hands and a palm cross that has been blessed. Eight days people arriving to pray. And on the ninth day, the cross of lime and sand raised, and my named called out—Inés Alfaro. The twisted neck of a rooster. Pork tamales wrapped in corn leaves. The masqueraders dancing, the men dressed as women, the women as men. Violins, guitars, one loud drum.

And I see other faces and other lives. My mother in a field of *cempoaxúchitl* flowers with a man who is not my father. Her *rebozo de bolita* spread beneath them. The smell of crushed grass and garlic. How, at a signal from her lover, the others descend. The clouds scurrying away. A machete-sharp cane stake greased with lard and driven into the earth. How the men gather my mother like a bundle of corn. Her sharp cry against the infinity of sky when the cane stake pierces her. How each waiting his turn grunts words like hail that splits open the skin, just as before they'd whispered words of love.

The star of her sex open to the sky. Clouds moving soundlessly, and the sky changing colors. Hours. Eyes still fixed on the clouds the morning they find her—braids undone, a man's *sombrero* tipped on her head, a cigar in her mouth, as if to say, this is what we do to women who try to act like men.

The small black bundle that is my mother delivered to my father's door. My father without a "who" or "how." He knows as well as everyone.

How the sky let go a storm of stones. The corn harvest ruined. And how we move from Tetelcingo to my Tía Chucha's in Cuautla.

And I see our children. Malenita with her twins, who will never marry, two brave *solteronas* living out their lives selling herbs in La Merced in Mexico City.

And our Nicolás, a grown man, the grief and shame

Nicolás will bring to the Zapata name when he kicks up a fuss about the parcel of land the government gives him, how it isn't enough, how it's never enough, how the son of a great man should not live like a peasant. The older Anenecuilcans shaking their heads when he sells the Zapata name to the PRI campaign.

And I see the ancient land titles the smoky morning they are drawn up in Náhuatl and recorded on tree-bark paper—*conceded to our pueblo the 25th of September of 1607 by the Viceroy of New Spain*—the land grants that prove the land has always been our land.

And I see that dappled afternoon in Anenecuilco when the government has begun to look for you. And I see you unearth the strong box buried under the main altar of the village church, and hand it to Chico Franco—*If you lose this, I'll have you dangling from the tallest tree,* compadre. *Not before they fill me with bullets,* Chico said and laughed.

And the evening, already as an old man, in the Canyon of the Wolves, Chico Franco running and running, old wolf, old cunning, the government men Nicolás sent shouting behind him, his sons Vírulo and Julián, young, crumpled on the cool courtyard tiles like bougainvillea blossoms, and how useless it all is, because the deeds are buried under the floorboards of a *pulquería* named La Providencia, and no one knowing where they are after the bullets pierce Chico's body. Nothing better or worse than before, and nothing the same or different.

And I see rivers of stars and the wide sea with its sad voice, and emerald fish fluttering on the sea bottom, glad to be themselves. And bell towers and blue forests, and a store window filled with hats. A burnt foot like the inside of a plum. A lice comb with two nits. The lace hem of a woman's dress. The violet smoke from a cigarette. A boy urinating into a tin. The milky eyes of a blind man. The chipped finger of a San Isidro statue. The tawny bellies of dark women giving life.

And more lives and more blood, those being born as well as those dying, the ones who ask questions and the ones who keep quiet, the days of grief and all the flower colors of joy.

Ay papacito, cielito de mi corazón, now the burros are complaining. The rooster beginning his cries. Morning already? Wait, I want to remember everything before you leave me.

How you looked at me in the San Lázaro plaza. How you kissed me under my father's avocado tree. Nights you loved me with a pleasure close to sobbing, how I stilled the trembling in your chest and held you, held you. Miliano, Milianito.

My sky, my life, my eyes. Let me look at you. Before you open those eyes of yours. The days to come, the days gone by. Before we go back to what we'll always be.

LITTLE MIRACLES, KEPT PROMISES

Exvoto Donated as Promised

On the 20th of December of 1988 we suffered a terrible disaster on the road to Corpus Christi. The bus we were riding skidded and overturned near Robstown and a lady and her little girl were killed. Thanks to La Virgen de Guadalupe we are alive, all of us miraculously unharmed, and with no visible scars, except we are afraid to ride buses. We dedicate this *retablo* to La Virgencita with our affection and gratitude and our everlasting faith.

Familia Arteaga
Alice, Texas
G.R. (Gracias Recibido/Thanks Given)

Blessed Santo Niño de Atocha,

Thank you for helping us when Chapa's truck got stolen. We didn't know how we was going to make it. He needs it to get to work, and this job, well, he's been on probation since we got him to quit drinking. Raquel and the kids are hardly ever afraid of him anymore, and we are proud parents. We don't know how we can repay you for everything you have done for our family. We will light a candle to you every Sunday and never forget you.

Sidronio Tijerina
Brenda A. Camacho de Tijerina
San Angelo, Texas

Dear San Martín de Porres,

Please send us clothes, furniture, shoes, dishes. We need anything that don't eat. Since the fire we have to start all over again and Lalo's disability check ain't much and don't go far. Zulema would like to finish school but I says she can just forget about it now. She's our oldest and her place is at home helping us out I told her. Please make her see some sense. She's all we got.

Thanking you,
Adelfa Vásquez
Escobas, Texas

Dear San Antonio de Padua,

Can you please help me find a man who isn't a pain in the *nalgas.* There aren't any in Texas, I swear. Especially not in San Antonio.

Can you do something about all the educated Chicanos who have to go to California to find a job. I guess what my sister Irma says is true: "If you didn't get a husband when you were in college, you don't get one."

I would appreciate it very much if you sent me a man who speaks Spanish, who at least can pronounce his name the way it's supposed to be pronounced. Someone please who never calls himself "Hispanic" unless he's applying for a grant from Washington, D.C.

Can you send me a man man. I mean someone who's not ashamed to be seen cooking or cleaning or looking after himself. In other words, a man who acts like an adult. Not one who's never lived alone, never bought his own underwear, never ironed his own shirts, never even heated his own *tortillas.* In other words, don't send me someone like my brothers who my mother ruined with too much *chichi,* or I'll throw him back.

I'll turn your statue upside down until you send him to me. I've put up with too much too long, and now I'm just too intelligent, too powerful, too beautiful, too sure of who I am finally to deserve anything less.

Ms. Barbara Ybáñez
San Antonio, TX

Dear Niño Fidencio,

I would like for you to help me get a job with good pay, benefits, and retirement plan. I promise you if you help me I will make a pilgrimage to your tomb in Espinazo and bring you flowers. Many thanks.

César Escandón
Pharr, Tejas

DEAR DON PEDRITO JARAMILLO HEALER OF LOS OLMOS

MY NAME IS ENRIQUETA ANTONIA SANDOVAL I LIVE IN SAN MARCOS TX I AM SICK THEY OPERATED ME FROM A KIDNEY AND A TUMOR OF CANCER BUT THANKS

TO GOD I AM ALIVE BUT I HAVE TO GET TREATMENTS FOR A YEAR THE KIMO I AM 2½ YEARS OLD BUT MY GRANDMA BROUGHT ME THAT YOU AND OUR LORD WHO IS IN THE HEAVENS WILL CURE ME WITH THIS LETTER THAT I AM DEPOSITING HERE ITS MY GRANDMA WHO IS WRITING THIS I HOPE EVERYBODY WHO SEES THIS LETTER WILL TAKE A MINUTE TO ASK FOR MY HEALTH

ENRIQUETA ANTONIA SANDOVAL
2 AND A HALF YEARS OLD

I LEOCADIA DIMAS VDA. DE CORDERO OF SAN MARCOS TX HAVE COME TO PAY THIS REQUEST TO DON PEDRITO THAT MY GRANDDAUGHTER WILL COME OUT FINE FROM HER OPERATION THANKS TO GOD AND THOSE WHO HELPED SUCH GOOD DOCTORS THAT DID THEIR JOB WELL THE REST IS IN GODS HANDS THAT HE DO HIS WILL MANY THANKS WITH ALL MY HEART.

YOUR VERY RESPECTFUL SERVANT
LEOCADIA

Oh Mighty Poderosos, Blessed Powerful Ones,

You who are crowned in heaven and who are so close to our Divine Savior, I implore your intercession before the Almighty on my behalf. I ask for peace of spirit and prosperity, and that the demons in my path that are the cause of all my woes be removed so that they no longer torment me. Look favorably on this petition and bless me, that I may continue to glorify your deeds with all my heart—*santísimo* Niño Fidencio, *gran* General Pancho Villa, *bendito*

Don Pedrito Jaramillo, *virtuoso* John F. Kennedy, and blessed Pope John Paul. Amen.

Gertrudis Parra
Uvalde, Tejas

Father Almighty,

Teach me to love my husband again. Forgive me.

s.
Corpus Christi

Seven African Powers that surround our Savior—Obatalá, Yemayá, Ochún, Orula, Ogún, Eleguá, and Shangó—why don't you behave and be good to me? Oh Seven African Powers, come on, don't be bad. Let my Illinois lottery ticket win, and if it does, don't let my cousin Cirilo in Chicago cheat me out of my winnings, since I'm the one who pays for the ticket and all he does is buy it for me each week—if he does even that. He's my cousin, but like the Bible says, better to say nothing than to say nothing nice.

Protect me from the evil eye of the envious and don't let my enemies do me harm, because I've never done a thing wrong to anyone first. Save this good Christian who the wicked have taken advantage of.

Seven Powers, reward my devotion with good luck. Look after me, why don't you? And don't forget me because I never forget you.

Moises Ildefonso Mata
San Antonio, Texas

Virgencita de Guadalupe,

I promise to walk to your shrine on my knees the very first day I get back, I swear, if you will only get the Tortillería la Casa de la Masa to pay me the $253.72 they owe me for two weeks' work. I put in 67½ hours that first week and 79 hours the second, and I don't have anything to show for it yet. I calculated with the taxes deducted, I have $253.72 coming to me. That's all I'm asking for. The $253.72 I have coming to me.

I have asked the proprietors Blanquita and Rudy Mondragón, and they keep telling me next week, next week, next week. And it's almost the middle of the third week already and I don't know how I'm going to do it to pay this week's rent, since I'm already behind, and the other guys have loaned me as much as they're able, and I don't know what I'm going to do, I don't know what I'm going to do.

My wife and the kids and my in-laws all depend on what I send home. We are humble people, Virgencita. You know I'm not full of vices. That's how I am. It's been hard for me to live here so far away without seeing my wife, you know. And sometimes one gets tempted, but no, and no, and no. I'm not like that. Please, Virgencita, all I'm asking for is my $253.72. There is no one else I can turn to here in this country, and well, if you can't help me, well, I just don't know.

Arnulfo Contreras
San Antonio, Tejas

Saint Sebastian who was persecuted with arrows and then survived, thank you for answering my prayers! All them arrows that had persecuted me—my brother-in-law

Ernie and my sister Alba and their kids—el Junior, la Gloria, and el Skyler—all gone. And now my home sweet home is mine again, and my Dianita bien lovey-dovey, and my kids got something to say to me besides who hit who.

Here is the little gold *milagrito* I promised you, a little house, see? And it ain't that cheap gold-plate shit either. So now that I paid you back, we're even, right? Cause I don't like for no one to say Victor Lozano don't pay his debts. I pays cash on the line, bro. And Victor Lozano's word like his deeds is solid gold.

Victor A. Lozano
Houston, TX

Dear San Lázaro,

My mother's *comadre* Demetria said if I prayed to you that like maybe you could help me because you were raised from the dead and did a lot of miracles and maybe if I lit a candle every night for seven days and prayed, you might maybe could help me with my face breaking out with so many pimples. Thank you.

Rubén Ledesma
Hebbronville, Texas

Santísima Señora de San Juan de los Lagos,

We came to see you twice when they brought you to San Antonio, my mother and my sister Yolanda and two of my aunts, Tía Enedina and my Tía Perla, and we drove all the way from Beeville just to visit you and make our requests.

I don't know what my Tía Enedina asked for, she's always so secretive, but probably it had to do with her son

Beto who doesn't do anything but hang around the house and get into trouble. And my Tía Perla no doubt complained about her ladies' problems—her ovaries that itch, her tangled fallopians, her uterus that makes her seasick with all its flipping and flopping. And Mami who said she only came along for the ride, lit three candles so you would bless us all and sweep jealousy and bitterness from our hearts because that's what she says every day and every night. And my sister Yoli asked that you help her lose weight because *I don't want to wind up like Tía Perla, embroidering altar cloths and dressing saints.*

But that was a year ago, Virgencita, and since then my cousin Beto was fined for killing the neighbor's rooster with a flying Big Red bottle, and my Tía Perla is convinced her uterus has fallen because when she walks something inside her rattles like a maraca, and my mother and my aunts are arguing and yelling at each other same as always. And my stupid sister Yoli is still sending away for even stupider products like the Grasa Fantástica, guaranteed to burn away fat—*It really works, Tere, just rub some on while you're watching TV*—only she's fatter than ever and just as sad.

What I realize is that we all made the trip to San Antonio to ask something of you, Virgencita, we all needed you to listen to us. And of all of us, my mama and sister Yoli, and my aunts Enedina and Perla, of all of us, you granted me my petition and sent, just like I asked, a guy who would love only me because I was tired of looking at girls younger than me walking along the street or riding in cars or standing in front of the school with a guy's arm hooked around their neck.

So what is it I'm asking for? Please, Virgencita. Lift this heavy cross from my shoulders and leave me like I was before, wind on my neck, my arms swinging free, and no one telling me how I ought to be.

Teresa Galindo
Beeville, Texas

Miraculous Black Christ of Esquipulas,

Please make our grandson to be nice to us and stay away from drugs. Save him to find a job and move away from us. Thank you.

Grandma y Grandfather
Harlingen

M3r1c5l45s Bl1ck Chr3st 4f 2sq53p5l1s,

3 1sk y45, L4rd, w3th 1ll my h21rt pl21s2 w1tch 4v2r M1nny B2n1v3d2s wh4 3s 4v2rs21s. 3 l4v2 h3m 1nd 3 d4n't kn4w wh1t t4 d4 1b45t 1ll th3s l4v2 s1dn2ss 1nd sh1m2 th1t f3lls m2.

B2nj1m3n T.
D2l R34 TX

Milagroso Cristo Negro de Esquipulas,

Te ofrezco este retrato de mis niños. Wáchelos, Dios Santo, y si le quitas el trago a mi hijo te prometo prender velitas. Ayúdanos con nuestras cuentas, Señor, y que el cheque del income tax nos llegue pronto para pagar los biles. Danos una buena vida y que les ayudes a mis hijos a cambiar sus modos. Tú que eres tan bondadoso escucha estas peticiones que te pido con todo mi corazón y con toda la fe de mi alma. Ten piedad, Padre mio. Mi nombre es Adela O.

Elizondo.
Cotulla TX

Milagroso Cristo Negro,

Thank you por *el milagro de haber graduado* de high school. *Aquí le regalo mi retrato* de graduation.

Fito Moroles
Rockport, Texas

Cristo Negro,

Venimos desde muy lejos. Infinitas gracias, Señor. Gracias por habernos escuchado.

Familia Armendáriz G.
Matamoros, Tamps. México

Jesus Christ,

Please keep Deborah Abrego and Ralph S. Urrea together forever.

Love,
Deborah Abrego
Sabinal, Texas

Blessed Virgen de los Remedios,

Señora Dolores Alcalá de Corchado finds herself gravely ill from a complication that resulted after a delicate operation she underwent Thursday last, and from which she was recovering satisfactorily until suffering a hemmorhage Tuesday morning. Please intercede on her behalf. We leave her in the hands of God, that His will be done, now that we have witnessed her suffering and don't know whether she should die or continue this life. Her husband of forty-eight years offers this request with all his heart.

Señor Gustavo Corchado B.
Laredo, Tejas

Madrecita de Dios,

Thank you. Our child is born healthy!

Rene y Janie Garza
Hondo, TX

Saint Jude, patron saint of lost causes,

Help me pass my English 320, British Restoration Literature class and everything to turn out ok.

Eliberto González
Dallas

Virgencita . . .

I've cut off my hair just like I promised I would and pinned my braid here by your statue. Above a Toys "Я" Us name tag that says IZAURA. Along several hospital bracelets. Next to a business card for Sergio's Casa de la Belleza Beauty College. Domingo Reyna's driver's license. Notes printed on the flaps of envelopes. Silk roses, plastic roses, paper roses, roses crocheted out of fluorescent orange yarn. Photo button of a baby in a *charro* hat. Caramel-skinned women in a white graduation cap and gown. Mean dude in bandanna and tattoos. Oval black-and-white passport portrait of the sad uncle who never married. A mama in a sleeveless dress watering the porch plants. Sweet boy with new mustache and new soldier uniform. Teenager with a little bit of herself sitting on her lap. Blurred husband and wife leaning one into the other as if joined at the hip. Black-and-white photo of the cousins *la* Josie *y la* Mary Helen, circa 1942. Polaroid of Sylvia Rios, First Holy Communion, age nine years.

So many *milagritos* safety-pinned here, so many little miracles dangling from red thread—a gold Sacred Heart, a tiny copper arm, a kneeling man in silver, a bottle, a brass truck, a foot, a house, a hand, a baby, a cat, a breast, a tooth, a belly button, an evil eye. So many petitions, so many promises made and kept. And there is nothing I can give you except this braid of hair the color of coffee in a glass.

Chayo, what have you done! All that beautiful hair.

Chayito, how could you ruin in one second what your mother took years to create?

You might as well've plucked out your eyes like Saint Lucy. All that hair!

My mother cried, did I tell you? All that beautiful hair . . .

I've cut off my hair. Which I've never cut since the day I was born. The donkey tail in a birthday game. Something shed like a snakeskin.

My head as light as if I'd raised it from water. My heart buoyant again, as if before I'd worn el Sagrado Corazón in my open chest. I could've lit this entire church with my grief.

I'm a bell without a clapper. A woman with one foot in this world and one foot in that. A woman straddling both. This thing between my legs, this unmentionable.

I'm a snake swallowing its tail. I'm my history and my future. All my ancestors' ancestors inside my own belly. All my futures and all my pasts.

I've had to steel and hoard and hone myself. I've had to push the furniture against the door and not let you in.

What you doing sitting in there in the dark?

I'm thinking.

Thinking of what?

Just . . . thinking.

You're nuts. Chayo, ven a saludar. *All the relatives are here. You come out of there and be sociable.*

Do boys think, and girls daydream? Do only girls have to come out and greet the relatives and smile and be nice and *quedar bien?*

It's not good to spend so much time alone.

What she do in there all by herself? It don't look right.

Chayito, when you getting married? Look at your cousin Leticia. She's younger than you.

How many kids you want when you grow up?

When I become a mommy . . .

You'll change. You'll see. Wait till you meet Mr. Right.

Chayo, tell everybody what it is you're studying again.

Look at our Chayito. She likes making her little pictures. She's gonna be a painter.

A painter! Tell her I got five rooms that need painting.

When you become a mother . . .

Thank you for making all those months I held my breath not a child in my belly, but a thyroid problem in my throat.

I can't be a mother. Not now. Maybe never. Not for me to choose, like I didn't choose being female. Like I didn't choose being artist—it isn't something you choose. It's something you are, only I can't explain it.

I don't want to be a mother.

I wouldn't mind being a father. At least a father could still be artist, could love some*thing* instead of some*one,* and no one would call that selfish.

I leave my braid here and thank you for believing what I do is important. Though no one else in my family, no other woman, neither friend nor relative, no one I know, not even the heroine in the *telenovelas,* no woman wants to live alone.

I do.

Virgencita de Guadalupe. For a long time I wouldn't let you in my house. I couldn't see you without seeing my ma each time my father came home drunk and yelling, blaming everything that ever went wrong in his life on her.

I couldn't look at your folded hands without seeing my *abuela* mumbling, "My son, my son, my son . . ." Couldn't look at you without blaming you for all the pain my mother and her mother and all our mothers' mothers have put up with in the name of God. Couldn't let you in my house.

I wanted you bare-breasted, snakes in your hands. I wanted you leaping and somersaulting the backs of bulls. I wanted you swallowing raw hearts and rattling volcanic ash. I wasn't going to be my mother or my grandma. All that self-sacrifice, all that silent suffering. Hell no. Not here. Not me.

Don't think it was easy going without you. Don't think I didn't get my share of it from everyone. Heretic. Atheist. *Malinchista. Hocicona.* But I wouldn't shut my yap. My mouth always getting me in trouble. *Is* that *what they teach you at the university? Miss High-and-Mighty. Miss Thinks-She's-Too-Good-for-Us.* Acting like a *bolilla,* white girl. *Malinche.* Don't think it didn't hurt being called a traitor. Trying to explain to my ma, to my *abuela,* why I didn't want to be like them.

I don't know how it all fell in place. How I finally understood who you are. No longer Mary the mild, but our mother Tonantzín. Your church at Tepeyac built on the site of her temple. Sacred ground no matter whose goddess claims it.

That you could have the power to rally a people when a country was born, and again during civil war, and during a farmworkers' strike in California made me think maybe there is power in my mother's patience, strength in my grandmother's endurance. Because those who suffer have a special power, don't they? The power of understanding someone else's pain. And understanding is the beginning of healing.

When I learned your real name is Coatlaxopeuh, She Who Has Dominion over Serpents, when I recognized you as Tonantzín, and learned your names are Teteoinnan,

Toci, Xochiquetzal, Tlazolteotl, Coatlicue, Chalchiuhtlicue, Coyolxauhqui, Huixtocihuatl, Chicomecoatl, Cihuacoatl, when I could see you as Nuestra Señora de la Soledad, Nuestra Señora de los Remedios, Nuestra Señora del Perpetuo Socorro, Nuestra Señora de San Juan de los Lagos, Our Lady of Lourdes, Our Lady of Mount Carmel, Our Lady of the Rosary, Our Lady of Sorrows, I wasn't ashamed, then, to be my mother's daughter, my grandmother's granddaughter, my ancestors' child.

When I could see you in all your facets, all at once the Buddha, the Tao, the true Messiah, Yahweh, Allah, the Heart of the Sky, the Heart of the Earth, the Lord of the Near and Far, the Spirit, the Light, the Universe, I could love you, and, finally, learn to love me.

Mighty Guadalupana Coatlaxopeuh Tonantzín,

What "little miracle" could I pin here? Braid of hair in its place and know that I thank you.

Rosario (Chayo) De Leon
Austin, Tejas

YOU BRING OUT THE MEXICAN IN ME

You bring out the Mexican in me.
The hunkered thick dark spiral.
The core of a heart howl.
The bitter bile.
The tequila *lágrimas* on Saturday all
through next weekend Sunday.
You are the one I'd let go the other loves for,
surrender my one-woman house.
Allow you red wine in bed,
even with my vintage lace linens.
Maybe. Maybe.

For you.

You bring out the Dolores del Río in me.
The Mexican spitfire in me.
The raw *navajas,* glint and passion in me.
The raise Cain and dance with the rooster-footed devil
in me.

The spangled sequin in me.
The eagle and serpent in me.
The *mariachi* trumpets of the blood in me.
The Aztec love of war in me.
The fierce obsidian of the tongue in me.
The *berrinchuda, bien-cabrona* in me.
The Pandora's curiosity in me.
The pre-Columbian death and destruction in me.
The rainforest disaster, nuclear threat in me.
The fear of fascists in me.
Yes, you do. Yes, you do.

You bring out the colonizer in me.
The holocaust of desire in me.
The Mexico City '85 earthquake in me.
The Popocatépetl/Iztaccíhuatl in me.
The tidal wave of recession in me.
The Agustín Lara hopeless romantic in me.
The *barbacoa taquitos* on Sunday in me.
The cover the mirrors with cloth in me.

Sweet twin. My wicked other,
I am the memory that circles your bed nights,
that tugs you taut as moon tugs ocean.
I claim you all mine,
arrogant as Manifest Destiny.
I want to rattle and rent you in two.
I want to defile you and raise hell.
I want to pull out the kitchen knives,
dull and sharp, and whisk the air with crosses.
Me sacas lo mexicana en mí,
like it or not, honey.

You bring out the Uled-Nayl in me.
The stand-back-white-bitch in me.
The switchblade in the boot in me.
The Acapulco cliff diver in me.
The *Flecha Roja* mountain disaster in me.
The *dengue* fever in me.
The *¡Alarma!* murderess in me.
I could kill in the name of you and think
it worth it. Brandish a fork and terrorize rivals,
female and male, who loiter and look at you,
languid in your light. Oh,

I am evil. I am the filth goddess Tlazoltéotl.
I am the swallower of sins.
The lust goddess without guilt.
The delicious debauchery. You bring out
the primordial exquisiteness in me.
The nasty obsession in me.
The corporal and venial sin in me.
The original transgression in me.

Red ocher. Yellow ocher. Indigo. Cochineal.
Piñón. Copal. Sweetgrass. Myrrh.
All you saints, blessed and terrible,
Virgen de Guadalupe, diosa Coatlicue,
I invoke you.

Quiero ser tuya. Only yours. Only you.
Quiero amarte. Atarte. Amarrarte.
Love the way a Mexican woman loves. Let
me show you. Love the only way I know how.

YOU LIKE TO GIVE AND WATCH ME MY PLEASURE

You like to give and watch me my
pleasure. Machete me in two.
Take for the taking what is yours.
This is how you like to have me.

I'm as naked as a field of cane,
as alone as all of Cuba
before you.

You could descend like rain,
destroy like fire
if you chose to.

If you chose to.

I could rise like *huracán*.
I could erupt as sudden as
a coup d'état of trumpets,
the sleepless eye of ocean,

a sky of black *urracas.*
If I chose to.

I don't choose to.
I let myself be taken.

This power is my gift to you.

LOVE POEM FOR A NON-BELIEVER

Because I miss
you I run my hand
along the flat of my thigh
curve of the hip
mango of the ass Imagine
it your hand across
the thrum of ribs
arpeggio of the breasts
collarbones you adore
that I don't

My neck is thin
You could cup
it with one hand
Yank the life from me
if you wanted

I've cut my hair
You can't tug

my hair anymore
A jet of black
through the fingers now

Your hands cool
along the jaw
skin of the eyelids
nape of the neck
soft as a mouth

And when we open like apple
split each other in half and
have seen the heart
of the heart
of the heart that part
you don't I don't
show anyone the part
we want to reel

back as soon as it
is suddenly unreeled like silk
flag or the prayer call
of a Mohammed we won't
have a word for this except
perhaps religion

I AM SO DEPRESSED I FEEL LIKE JUMPING IN THE RIVER BEHIND MY HOUSE BUT WON'T BECAUSE I'M THIRTY-EIGHT AND NOT EIGHTEEN

Bring me a drink.
I need to think a little.
Paper. Pen.
And I could use the stink
of a good cigar—even
though the sun's out.
The grackles in the trees.
The grackles inside my heart.
Broken feathers and stiff wings.

I could jump.
But I don't.
You could kill me.
But you won't.

The grackles
calling to each other.
The long hours.
The long hours.
The long hours.

NIGHT MADNESS POEM

There's a poem in my head
like too many cups of coffee.
A pea under twenty eiderdowns.
A sadness in my heart like stone.
A telephone. And always my
night madness that outs like bats
across this Texas sky.

I'm the crazy lady they warned you about.
The she of rumor talked about—
and worse, who talks.

It's no secret.
I'm here. Under a circle of light.
The light always on, resisting a glass,
an easy cigar. The kind

who reels the twilight sky.
Swoop circling.

I'm witch woman high
on tobacco and holy water.

I'm a woman delighted with her disasters.
They give me something to do.
A profession of sorts.
Keeps me industrious
and of some serviceable use.

In dreams the origami of the brain
opens like a fist, a pomegranate,
an expensive geometry.

Not true.
I haven't a clue
why I'm rumpled tonight.

Choose your weapon.
Mine—the telephone, my tongue.
Both black as a gun.

I have the magic of words,
the power to charm and kill at will.
To kill myself or to aim haphazardly.
And kill you.

I AM ON MY WAY TO OKLAHOMA TO BURY THE MAN I NEARLY LEFT MY HUSBAND FOR

Your name doesn't matter.
I loved you.
We loved.
The years

                I waited
by the river for your pickup
truck to find me. Footprints
scattered in the yellow sand.
Husband, mother-
in-law, kids wondering
where I'd gone.

                          You wouldn't
the years I begged. Would
the years I wouldn't. Only
one of us had sense at a time.

I won't see you again.

I guess life presents you
choices and you choose. Smarter
over the years. Oh smarter.
The sensible thing smarting
over the years, the sensible
thing to excess, I guess.

My life—deed I have
done to artistic extreme—I
drag you with me. Must wake
early. Ride north tomorrow.
Send you off. Are you fine?
I think of you often, friend,
and fondly.

CLOUD

> If you are a poet, you will see clearly that there is a cloud floating in this sheet of paper.
>
> —*Thich Nhat Hanh*

Before you became a cloud, you were an ocean, roiled and murmuring like a mouth. You were the shadow of a cloud crossing over a field of tulips. You were the tears of a man who cried into a plaid handkerchief. You were a sky without a hat. Your heart puffed and flowered like sheets drying on a line.

And when you were a tree, you listened to trees and the tree things trees told you. You were the wind in the wheels of a red bicycle. You were the spidery *María* tattooed on the hairless arm of a boy in downtown Houston. You were the rain rolling off the waxy leaves of a magnolia tree. A lock of straw-colored hair wedged between the mottled pages of a Victor Hugo novel. A crescent of soap. A spider the color of a fingernail. The black net beneath the sea of olive trees. A skein of blue wool. A tea saucer wrapped in newspaper. An empty cracker tin. A bowl of blueberries in heavy cream. White wine in a green-stemmed glass.

And when you opened your wings to wind, across the punched-tin sky above a prison courtyard, those condemned to death and those condemned to life watched how smooth and sweet a white cloud glides.

TÚ QUE SABES DE AMOR

for Ito Romo

You come from that country
where the bitter is more bitter
and the sweet, sweeter.

You come from that town split
down the center like a cleft lip.
You come from the world
with a river running through it.
The dead. The living.
The river Styx.

You come from the twin Laredos.
Where the world was twice-named and
nopalitos flower like a ripe *ranchera.*
Ay, corazón, ¿tú que sabes de amor?

No wonder your heart is filled
with *mil peso* notes and *jacaranda.*

No wonder the clouds laugh each
time they cross without papers.

I know who you are.
You come from that country
where the bitter is more bitter
and the sweet, sweeter.

MEXICANS IN FRANCE

He says he likes Mexico.
Especially all that history.
That's what I understand
although my French
is not that good.

And wants to talk
about U.S. racism.
It's not often he meets
Mexicans in the south of France.

He remembers
a Mexican Marlon Brando once
on French tv.

How, in westerns,
the Mexicans are always
the bad guys. And—

Is it true
all Mexicans
carry knives?

I laugh.
—Lucky for you
I'm not carrying my knife
today.

He laughs too.
—I think
the knife you carry
is
abstract.

LOOSE WOMAN

They say I'm a beast.
And feast on it. When all along
I thought that's what a woman was.

They say I'm a bitch.
Or witch. I've claimed
the same and never winced.

They say I'm a *macha,* hell on wheels,
viva-la-vulva, fire and brimstone,
man-hating, devastating,
boogey-woman lesbian.
Not necessarily,
but I like the compliment.

The mob arrives with stones and sticks
to maim and lame and do me in.
All the same, when I open my mouth,
they wobble like gin.

Diamonds and pearls
tumble from my tongue.
Or toads and serpents.
Depending on the mood I'm in.

I like the itch I provoke.
The rustle of rumor
like crinoline.

I am the woman of myth and bullshit.
(True. I authored some of it.)
I built my little house of ill repute.
Brick by brick. Labored,
loved and masoned it.

I live like so.
Heart as sail, ballast, rudder, bow.
Rowdy. Indulgent to excess.
My sin and success—
I think of me to gluttony.

By all accounts I am
a danger to society.
I'm Pancha Villa.
I break laws,
upset the natural order,
anguish the Pope and make fathers cry.
I am beyond the jaw of law.
I'm *la desperada,* most-wanted public enemy.
My happy picture grinning from the wall.

I strike terror among the men.
I can't be bothered what they think.
¡Que se vayan a la ching chang chong!
For this, the cross, the calvary.
In other words, I'm anarchy.

I'm an aim-well,
shoot-sharp,
sharp-tongued,
sharp-thinking,
fast-speaking,
foot-loose,
loose-tongued,
let-loose,
woman-on-the-loose
loose woman.
Beware, honey.

I'm Bitch. Beast. *Macha.*
¡Wáchale!
Ping! Ping! Ping!
I break things.

VERDE, BLANCO, Y COLORADO

Uncle Fat-Face's brand-new used white Cadillac, Uncle Baby's green Impala, Father's red Chevrolet station wagon bought that summer on credit are racing to the Little Grandfather's and Awful Grandmother's house in Mexico City. Chicago, Route 66—Ogden Avenue past the giant Turtle Wax turtle—all the way to Saint Louis, Missouri, which Father calls by its Spanish name, San Luis. San Luis to Tulsa, Oklahoma. Tulsa, Oklahoma, to Dallas. Dallas to San Antonio to Laredo on 81 till we are on the other side. Monterrey. Saltillo. Matehuala. San Luis Potosí. Querétaro. Mexico City.

Every time Uncle Fat-Face's white Cadillac passes our red station wagon, the cousins—Elvis, Aristotle, and Byron—stick their tongues out at us and wave.

—Hurry, we tell Father.—Go faster!

When we pass the green Impala, Amor and Paz tug Uncle Baby's shoulder.—Daddy, please!

My brothers and I send them raspberries, we wag our tongues and make faces, we spit and point and laugh. The three cars—green Impala, white Cadillac, red station wagon—racing, passing each other sometimes on the shoulder of the road. Wives yelling, —Slower! Children yelling, —Faster!

What a disgrace when one of us gets carsick and we have to stop the car. The green Impala, the white Caddy whooshing past noisy and happy as a thousand flags. Uncle Fat-Face *toot-tooting* that horn like crazy.

CHILLANTE

—If we make it to Toluca, I'm walking to church on my knees.

Aunty Licha, Elvis, Aristotle, and Byron are hauling things out to the curb. Blenders. Transistor radios. Barbie dolls. Swiss Army knives. Plastic crystal chandeliers. Model airplanes. Men's button-down dress shirts. Lace push-up bras. Socks. Cut-glass necklaces with matching earrings. Hair clippers. Mirror sunglasses. Panty girdles. Ballpoint pens. Eye shadow kits. Scissors. Toasters. Acrylic pullovers. Satin quilted bedspreads. Towel sets. All this besides the boxes of used clothing.

Outside, roaring like the ocean, Chicago traffic from the Northwest and Congress Expressways. Inside, another roar; in Spanish from the kitchen radio, in English from TV cartoons, and in a mix of the two from her boys begging for, —*Un nikle* for Italian lemonade. But Aunty Licha doesn't hear anything. Under her breath Aunty is bargaining, —*Virgen Purísima,* if we even make it to Laredo, even that, I'll say three rosaries . . .

—*Cállate, vieja,* you make me nervous. Uncle Fat-Face

is fiddling with the luggage rack on top of the roof. It has taken him two days to get everything to fit inside the car. The white Cadillac's trunk is filled to capacity. The tires sag. The back half of the car dips down low. There isn't room for anything else except the passengers, and even so, the cousins have to sit on top of suitcases.

—Daddy, my legs hurt already.

—You. Shut your snout or you ride in the trunk.

—But there isn't any room in the trunk.

—I said shut your snout!

To pay for the vacation, Uncle Fat-Face and Aunty Licha always bring along items to sell. After visiting the Little Grandfather and Awful Grandmother in the city, they take a side trip to Aunty Licha's hometown of Toluca. All year their apartment looks like a store. A year's worth of weekends spent at Maxwell Street flea market* collecting merchandise for the trip south. Uncle says what sells is *lo chillante,* literally the screaming. —The gaudier the better, says the Awful Grandmother. —No use taking anything of value to that town of Indians.

*The original Maxwell Street, a Chicago flea market for more than 120 years, spread itself around the intersections of Maxwell and Halsted Streets. It was a filthy, pungent, wonderful place filled with astonishing people, good music, and goods from don't-ask-where. Devoured by the growth of the University of Illinois, it was relocated, though the new Maxwell Street market is no longer on Maxwell Street and exists as a shadow of its former grime and glory. Only Jim's Original Hot Dogs, founded in 1939, stands where it always has, a memorial to Maxwell Street's funky past.†

†Alas! While busy writing this book, Jim's Original Hot Dogs was gobbled up by the University of Illinois and Mayor Daley's gentrification; tidy parks and tidy houses for the very very wealthy, while the poor, as always, get swept under the rug, out of sight and out of mind.

Each summer it's something unbelievable that sells like *hot queques.* Topo Gigio key rings. Eyelash curlers. Wind Song perfume sets. Plastic rain bonnets. This year Uncle is betting on glow-in-the-dark yo-yos.

Boxes. On top of the kitchen cabinets and the refrigerator, along the hallway walls, behind the three-piece sectional couch, from floor to ceiling, on top or under things. Even the bathroom has a special storage shelf high above so no one can touch.

In the boys' room, floating near the ceiling just out of reach, toys nailed to the walls with upholstery tacks. Tonka trucks, model airplanes, Erector sets still in their original cardboard boxes with the cellophane window. They're not to play with, they're to look at. —This one I got last Christmas, and that one was a present for my seventh birthday . . . Like displays at a museum.

We've been waiting all morning for Uncle Fat-Face to telephone and say, —*Quihubo,* brother, *vámonos,* so that Father can call Uncle Baby and say the same thing. Every year the three Reyes sons and their families drive south to the Awful Grandmother's house on Destiny Street, Mexico City, one family at the beginning of the summer, one in the middle, and one at the summer's end.

—But what if something happens? the Awful Grandmother asks her husband.

—Why ask me, I'm already dead, the Little Grandfather says, retreating to his bedroom with his newspaper and his cigar. —You'll do what you want to do, same as always.

—What if someone falls asleep at the wheel like the time Concha Chacón became a widow and lost half her family near Dallas. What a barbarity! And did you hear that sad story about Blanca's cousins, eight people killed just as they were returning from Michoacán, right outside the Chicago city limits, a patch of ice and a light pole in some place called Aurora, *pobrecitos.* Or what about that station wagon full of gringa nuns that fell off the mountainside near Saltillo. But that was the old highway through the Sierra Madre before they built the new interstate.

All the same, we are too familiar with the roadside crosses and the stories they stand for. The Awful Grandmother complains so much, her sons finally give in. That's why this year Uncle Fat-Face, Uncle Baby, and Father—el Tarzán—finally agree to drive down together, although they never agree on anything.

—If you ask me, the whole idea stinks, Mother says, mopping the kitchen linoleum. She shouts from the kitchen to the bathroom, where Father is trimming his mustache over the sink.

—Zoila, why do you insist on being so stubborn? Father shouts into the mirror clouding the glass. —*Ya verás.* You'll see, *vieja,* it'll be fun.

—And stop calling me *vieja,* Mother shouts back. —I hate that word! I'm not old, your mother's old.

We're going to spend the entire summer in Mexico. We won't leave until school ends, and we won't come back until after it's started. Father, Uncle Fat-Face, and Uncle Baby don't have to report to the L. L. Fish Furniture Company on South Ashland until September.

—Because we're such good workers our boss gave us the whole summer off, imagine that.

But that's nothing but story. The three Reyes brothers have quit their jobs. When they don't like a job, they quit.

They pick up their hammers and say, —Hell you . . . Get outta . . . Full of *sheet.* They are craftsmen. They don't use a staple gun and cardboard like the upholsterers in the U.S. They make sofas and chairs *by hand.* Quality work. And when they don't like their boss, they pick up their hammers and their time cards and walk out cursing in two languages, with tacks in the soles of their shoes and lint in their beard stubble and hair, and bits of string dangling from the hem of their sweaters.

But they didn't quit this time, did they? No, no. The real story is this. The bosses at the L. L. Fish Furniture Company on South Ashland have begun to dock the three because they arrive sixteen minutes after the hour, forty-three minutes, fifty-two, instead of on time. According to Uncle Fat-Face, —We *are* on time. It depends on which time you are on, Western time or the calendar of the sun. The L. L. Fish Furniture Company on South Ashland Avenue has decided they don't have time for the brothers Reyes anymore. —Go hell . . . What's a matter . . . Same to you mother!

It's the Awful Grandmother's idea that her *mijos* drive down to Mexico together. But years afterward everyone will forget and blame each other.

MEXICO NEXT RIGHT

Not like on the Triple A atlas from orange to pink, but at a stoplight in a rippled heat and a dizzy gasoline stink, the United States ends all at once, a tangled shove of red lights from cars and trucks waiting their turn to get past the bridge. Miles and miles.

—Oh, my Got, Father says in his gothic English. —Holy cripes! says Mother, fanning herself with a Texaco road map.

I forgot the light, white and stinging like an onion. I remembered the bugs, a windshield spotted with yellow. I remembered the heat, a sun that melts into the bones like Bengay. I remembered how big Texas is. —Are we in Mexico yet? —No, not yet. [Sleep, wake up.] —Are we in Mexico yet? —Still Texas. [Sleep, wake up.] —Are we . . . —Christ Almighty!!!

But the light. That I don't remember forgetting until I remember it.

We've crossed Illinois, Missouri, Oklahoma, and Texas singing all the songs we know. "The Moon Men Mambo" from our favorite Rocky and Bullwinkle album. *Ah, ah, aaaah! Scrooch, doobie-doobie, doobie-do. Swing your partner from planet to planet when you dooooo the moon man mamboooo!* The *Yogi Bear* song. *He will sleep till noon, but before it's dark he'll have ev'ry picnic basket that's in Jellystone Park . . .* We sing TV commercials. *Get the blanket with the A, you can trust the big red A. Get the blanket made with ACRYLAN today . . . Knock on any Norge, knock on any Norge, hear the secret sound of quality, knock on any Norge! Years from now you'll be glad you chose Norge. CoCo Wheats, CoCo Wheats can't be beat. It's the creamy hot cereal with the cocoa treat . . .* Until Mother yells, —Will you shut your *hocicos* or do I have to shut them for you?!!!

But crossing the border, nobody feels like singing. Everyone hot and sticky and in a bad mood, hair stiff from riding with the windows open, the backs of the knees sweaty, a little circle of spit next to where my head fell asleep; "good lucky" Father thought to sew beach towel slipcovers for our new car.

No more billboards announcing the next Stuckey's candy store, no more truck-stop donuts or roadside picnics with bologna-and-cheese sandwiches and cold bottles of 7-Up. Now we'll drink fruit-flavored sodas, tamarind, apple, pineapple; Pato Pascual with Donald Duck on the bottle, or Lulú, Betty Boop soda, or the one we hear on the radio, the happy song for Jarritos soda.

As soon as we cross the bridge everything switches to another language. *Toc,* says the light switch in this country, at home it says *click. Honk,* say the cars at home, here they say *tán-tán-tán.* The *scrip-scrape-scrip* of high heels across *saltillo* floor tiles. The angry lion growl of the corrugated curtains when the shopkeepers roll them open each morning and the lazy lion roar at night when they pull them shut. The *pic, pic, pic* of somebody's faraway hammer. Church bells over and over, all day, even when it's not o'clock. Roosters. The hollow echo of a dog barking. Bells from skinny horses pulling tourists in a carriage, *clip-clop* on cobblestones and big chunks of horse *caquita* tumbling out of them like shredded wheat.

Sweets sweeter, colors brighter, the bitter more bitter. A cage of parrots all the rainbow colors of Lulú sodas. Pushing a window out to open it instead of pulling it up. A cold slash of door latch in your hand instead of the dull round doorknob. Tin sugar spoon and how surprised the hand feels because it's so light. Children walking to school in the morning with their hair still wet from the morning bath.

Mopping with a stick and a purple rag called *la jerga* instead of a mop. The fat lip of a soda pop bottle when you tilt your head back and drink. Birthday cakes walking out of a bakery without a box, just like that, on a wooden plate. And the metal tongs and tray when you buy Mexican sweet bread, help yourself. Cornflakes served with *hot* milk! A balloon painted with wavy pink stripes wearing a paper hat. A milk gelatin with a fly like a little black raisin rubbing its hands. Light and heavy, loud and soft, *thud* and *ting* and *ping.*

Churches the color of *flan.* Vendors selling slices of *jícama* with *chile,* lime juice, and salt. Balloon vendors. The vendor of flags. The corn-on-the-cob vendor. The pork rind vendor. The fried-banana vendor. The pancake vendor. The vendor of strawberries in cream. The vendor of rainbow *pirulís,* of apple bars, of *tejocotes* bathed in caramel.

The meringue man. The ice cream vendor, —A very good ice cream at two *pesos.* The coffee man with the coffeemaker on his back and a paper cup dispenser, the cream-and-sugar boy scuttling alongside him.

Little girls in Sunday dresses like lace bells, like umbrellas, like parachutes, the more lace and froufrou the better. Houses painted purple, electric blue, tiger orange, aquamarine, a yellow like a taxicab, hibiscus red with a yellow-and-green fence. Above doorways, faded wreaths from an anniversary or a death till the wind and rain erase them. A woman in an apron scrubbing the sidewalk in front of her house with a pink plastic broom and a bright green bucket filled with suds. A workman carrying a long metal pipe on his shoulder, whistling *ffftttt-fffftttt* to warn people—Watch out!—the pipe longer than he is tall, almost putting out someone's eye, *ya mero*—but he doesn't, does he? *Ya mero, pero no.* Almost, but not quite. *Sí, pero no.* Yes, but no.

Fireworks displays, *piñata* makers, palm weavers. Pens, —Five different styles, they cost us a lot! A restaurant called "His Majesty, the Taco." The napkins, little triangles of hard paper with the name printed on one side. Breakfast: a basket of *pan dulce,* Mexican sweet bread; hotcakes with honey; or steak; *frijoles* with fresh *cilantro; molletes;* or scrambled eggs with *chorizo;* eggs *a la mexicana* with tomato, onion, and *chile;* or *huevos rancheros.* Lunch: lentil soup; fresh-baked crusty *bolillos;* carrots with lime juice; *carne asada;* abalone; *tortillas.* Because we are sitting outdoors, Mexican dogs under the Mexican tables. —I can't stand dogs under the table when I'm eating, Mother complains, but as soon as we shoo two away, four others trot over.

The smell of diesel exhaust, the smell of somebody

roasting coffee, the smell of hot corn *tortillas* along with the *pat-pat* of the women's hands making them, the sting of roasting *chiles* in your throat and in your eyes. Sometimes a smell in the morning, very cool and clean that makes you sad. And a night smell when the stars open white and soft like fresh *bolillo* bread.

Every year I cross the border, it's the same—my mind forgets. But my body always remembers.

TARZAN

We come in all sizes, from little to big, like a xylophone. Rafa, Ito, Tikis, Toto, Lolo, Memo, and Lala. Rafael, Refugio, Gustavo, Alberto, Lorenzo, Guillermo, and Celaya. Rafa, Ito, Tikis, Toto, Lolo, Memo, *y* Lala. The younger ones couldn't say the older ones' names, and that's how Refugito became Ito, or Gustavito became Tikis, Alberto—Toto, Lorenzo—Lolo, Guillermo—Memo, and me, Celaya—Lala. Rafa, Ito, Tikis, Toto, Lolo, Memo, *y* Lala. When the Grandmother calls us she says, —*Tú*. Or sometimes, —*Oyes, tú*.

Elvis, Aristotle, and Byron are Uncle Fat-Face and Aunty Licha's. The Grandmother says to Uncle Fat-Face, —How backwards that Licha naming those poor babies after anyone she finds in her horoscopes. Thank God Shakespeare was stillborn. Can you imagine answering to "Shakespeare Reyes"? What a beating life would've given him. Too sad to think your father lost three of his ribs in the war so that his grandchild could be named Elvis . . . Don't pretend you don't know! . . . Elvis Presley is a national enemy . . . He is . . . Why would I make it up? When he was making that movie in Acapulco he said, "The last thing I want to do in my life is kiss a Mexican." That's what he said, I swear it. Kiss a Mexican. It was in all the papers. What was Licha thinking!

—But our Elvis was born seven years ago, Mother. How was Licha to know Elvis Presley would come to Mexico and say such things?

—Well, someone should've thought about the future, eh? And now look. The whole republic is boycotting that pig, and my grandchild is named Elvis! What a barbarity!

Amor and Paz are Uncle Baby and Aunty Ninfa's, named "Love" and "Peace" because, —We were happy God sent us such pretty little girls. They're so evil they stick their tongues out at us while their father is saying this.

Like always, when we first arrive at the Grandparents' house, my brothers and I are shy and speak only to one another, in English, which is rude. But by the second day we upset our cousin Antonieta Araceli, who is not used to the company of kids. We break her old Cri-Crí* records. We lose the pieces to her Turista game. We use too much toilet paper, or at other times too little. We stick our dirty fingers in the bowl of beans soaking for the midday meal. We run up and down the stairs and across the courtyard chasing each other through the back apartments where the Grandparents, Aunty Light-Skin, and Antonieta Araceli live, and through the front apartments where we stay.

*Before Jiminy Cricket, there was Cri-Crí, the Singing Cricket, the alter ego of that brilliant children's composer Francisco Gabilondo Soler, who created countless songs, influencing generations of children and would-be poets across *América Latina*.

We like being seen on the roof, like house servants, without so much as thinking what passersby might mistake us for. We try sneaking into the Grandparents' bedroom when no one is looking, which the Awful Grandmother strictly forbids. All this we do and more. Antonieta Araceli faithfully reports as much to the Awful Grandmother, and the Awful Grandmother herself has seen how these children raised on the other side don't know enough to answer, —*¿Mande usted?* to their elders. —What? we say in the horrible language, which the Awful Grandmother hears as *¿Guat?* —What? we repeat to each other and to her. The Awful Grandmother shakes her head and mutters, —My daughters-in-law have given birth to a generation of monkeys.

Mi gorda, my chubby, is what Aunty Light-Skin calls her daughter, Antonieta Araceli. It was her baby name and cute when she was little, but not cute now because Antonieta Araceli is as thin as a shadow. —*¡Mi gorda!*

—Mama, please! When are you going to stop calling me that in front of everybody?

She means in front of us. Antonieta Araceli has decided she's a grown-up this summer and spends all day in front of the mirror plucking her eyebrows and mustache, but she's no grown-up. She's only two months younger than Rafa—thirteen. When the adults aren't around we shout, —*¡Mi gorda! ¡Mi gorda!* until she throws something at us.

—How did you get named Antonieta Araceli, what a funny name?

—It's not a funny name. I was named after a Cuban dancer who dances in the movies wearing beautiful outfits. Didn't you ever hear of María Antonieta Pons? She's famous and everything. Blond-blond-blond and white-white-white. Very pretty, not like you.

The Awful Grandmother calls Father *mijo. Mijo.* My son. —*Mijo, mijo.* She doesn't call Uncle Fat-Face or Uncle Baby *mijo,* even though they're her sons too. She calls them by their real names, —Federico. Or, —Armando—when she is angry, or their nicknames when she is not. —Fat-Face, Baby! —It's that when I was a baby I had a fat face, explains Uncle Fat-Face. —It's that I'm the youngest, says Uncle Baby. As if the Awful Grandmother doesn't notice Uncle Fat-Face isn't fat anymore and Uncle Baby isn't a baby. —It doesn't matter, says the Awful Grandmother. —All my sons are my sons. They're just as they were when they were little. I love them all the same, just enough but not too much. She uses the Spanish word *hijos,* which means sons and children all at once. —And your daughter? I ask. —What about her? The Awful Grandmother gives me that look, as if I'm a pebble in her shoe.

Aunty Light-Skin's real name is Norma, but who would think to call her that? She's always been known as la Güera even when she was a teeny tiny baby because, —Well, just look at her.

The Awful Grandmother is the one whose name ought to be the Parrot because she talks too much and too loudly, who squawks from the courtyard up to the second-story bedrooms, from the bedrooms down to the kitchen, from the rooftop all through the neighborhood of La Villa, the hills of Tepeyac, the bell tower of la Basílica de la Virgen de Guadalupe, the twin volcanoes—the warrior prince Popocatépetl, the sleeping princess Iztaccíhuatl.

Father's name is el Tarzán, Tío Tarzán to my cousins,

Uncle Tarzan, even though he doesn't look like Tarzan at all. In his bathing suit he looks like an Errol Flynn washed up on the beach, pale and skinny as a fish. But when Father was a little boy in Mexico he saw a Johnny Weissmuller movie at the neighborhood movie theater, The Flea. From that moment on, Father's life was changed. He jumped from a tree holding a branch, only the branch didn't hold. When his two broken arms were set and his mother cured from the fright she asked, —*¡Válgame Dios!* What got into you? Were you trying to kill yourself, or kill me? Answer!

How could Father answer? His heart was filled with so many wonders there were no words for. He wished to fly, he wanted to shout with the voice of the wind, he wanted to live in the sea of trees with the monkeys, satisfied picking each other's lice, glad to be shitting on people below. But how can one say this to one's mother?

Forever after Father was nicknamed el Tarzán by his *cuates.* Inocencio took his nickname in stride. El Tarzán was not so bad. Inocencio's best friend since the first grade was el Reloj, the Clock, because he was born with his left arm shorter than his right. At least Inocencio was not as unlucky as the neighbor who lost an ear in a knife fight and was, from that day till his death, called la Taza, the Cup. And what about the *pobre infeliz* who survived polio with a gimp foot, only to be named la Polka. *Pobrecito* el Moco, the Snot. El Pedo, the Fart. El Mojón, the Turd. Life was cruel. And hilarious all at once.

Juan el Chango. Beto la Guagua because he could not say *"agua"* when he was little. Meme el King Kong. Chale la Zorra. Balde la Mancha. El Vampiro. El Tlacuache. El Gallo. El Borrego. El Zorrillo. El Gato. El Mosco. El Conejo.

La Rana. El Pato. El Oso. La Ardilla. El Cuervo. El Pingüino. La Chicharra. El Tecolote. A whole menagerie of friends. When they saw each other at a soccer match, they'd shout, —There goes el Gallo over there. And instead of shouting, —Hey, Gallo!—they'd let loose a rooster crow—*kiki-riki-kiiiiiiii*—which would be answered by a Tarzan yell, or a bleat, or a bark, or a quack, or a hoot, or a shriek, or a buzz, or a caw.

SO HERE MY HISTORY BEGINS FOR YOUR GOOD UNDERSTANDING AND MY POOR TELLING

Once in the land of *los nopales,* before all the dogs were named after Woodrow Wilson, during that epoch when people still danced *el chotís, el cancán,* and *el vals* to a *violín, violoncelo,* and *salterio,* at the nose of a hill where a goddess appeared to an Indian, in that city founded when a serpent-devouring eagle perched on a cactus, beyond the twin volcanoes that were once prince and princess, under the sky and on the earth lived the woman Soledad and the man Narciso.

The woman Soledad is my Awful Grandmother. The man Narciso, my Little Grandfather. But as we begin this story they are simply themselves. They haven't bought the house on Destiny Street, number 12, yet. Nor have their sons been born and moved up north to that horrible country with its barbarian ways. Later, after my grandfather dies, my grandmother will come up north to live with us, until she suffers a terrible seizure that freezes her. Then she's left without words, except to stick the tip of her tongue between thin lips and sputter a frothy sentence of spit. So much left unsaid.

But this story is from the time of before. Before my Awful Grandmother became awful, before she became my father's mother. Once she had been a young woman who men looked at and women listened to. And before that she had been a girl.

Is there anyone alive who remembers the Awful Grandmother when she was a child? Is there anyone left in the world who once heard her call out "Mamá?" It was such a long, long time ago.

***¡Qué exagerada eres!* It wasn't that long ago!**

I have to exaggerate. It's just for the sake of the story. I need details. You never tell me anything.

And if I told you everything, what would there be for you to do, eh? I tell you just enough . . .

But not too much. Well, let me go on with the story, then.

And who's stopping you?

Soledad Reyes was a girl of good family, albeit humble, the daughter of famed *reboceros* from Santa María del Río, San Luis Potosí, where the finest shawls in all the republic come from, *rebozos* so light and thin they can be pulled through a wedding ring.

Her father, my great-grandfather Ambrosio Reyes, was a man who stank like a shipyard and whose fingernails were permanently stained blue. To tell the truth, the stink was not his fault. It was due to his expertise as a maker of black shawls, because black is the most difficult color to dye. The cloth must be soaked over and over in water where rusty skillets, pipes, nails, horseshoes, bed rails, chains, and wagon wheels have been left to dissolve.

Careful! Just enough, but not too much . . .

. . . Otherwise the cloth disintegrates and all the work is for nothing. So prized was the black *rebozo de olor,* it was said when the crazed ex-empress Carlota* was presented with one in her prison-castle in Belgium, she sniffed the cloth and joyously announced, —Today we leave for Mexico.

Just enough, but not too much.

Everyone in the world agreed Ambrosio Reyes' black shawls were the most exquisite anyone had ever seen, as black as Coyotepec pottery, as black as *huitlacoche,* the corn mushroom, as true-black as an *olla* of fresh-cooked black beans. But it was his wife Guillermina's fingers that gave

*The doomed empress Charlotte was the daughter of King Leopold of Belgium and wife to the well-meaning but foolish Austrian, the Archduke Maximilian of Hapsburg. Emperor Maximiliano and Empress Carlota were installed as rulers of Mexico in 1864 by disgruntled Mexican conservatives and clergy who believed foreign intervention would stabilize Mexico after the disastrous years of Santa Anna, who, as we recall, gave away half of Mexico to the United States. The puppet monarchs ruled for a few years, convinced that the Mexican people wanted them as their rulers—until the natives grew restless and France withdrew its troops.

Carlota left for Europe to seek Napoleon III's assistance, since he had promised to support them, but France had enough problems. He refused to see her. Abandoned and delirious, Carlota suffered a mental collapse and began to suspect everyone of trying to poison her. In desperation, she tried to enlist the aid of Pope Pius IX, and is the only woman "on record" to have spent the night at the Vatican, refusing to leave because she insisted it was the only safe refuge from Napoleon's assassins.

Meanwhile, back in Mexico, Maximiliano was executed by firing squad outside of Querétaro in 1866. Carlota was finally persuaded to return to her family in Belgium, where she lived exiled in a moated castle until her death in 1927 at the age of eighty-six.

I forgot to mention, Maximiliano was ousted by none other than Benito Juárez, the only pure-blooded Indian to rule Mexico. For a Hollywood version of the aforementioned, see *Juarez,* John Huston's 1939 film with the inestimable Bette Davis playing—who else—the madwoman.

the shawls their high value because of the fringe knotted into elaborate designs.

The art of *las empuntadoras* is so old no one remembers whether it arrived from the east, from the *macramé* of Arabia through Spain, or from the west from the blue-sky bay of Acapulco where galleons bobbed weighted down with the fine porcelain, lacquerware, and expensive silk of Manila and China. Perhaps, as is often the case with things Mexican, it came from neither and both.† Guillermina's signature design, with its intricate knots looped into interlocking figure eights, took one hundred and forty-six hours to complete, but if you asked her how she did it, she'd say, —How should I know? It's my hands that know, not my head.

Guillermina's mother had taught her the *empuntadora*'s art of counting and dividing the silk strands, of braiding and knotting them into fastidious rosettes, arcs, stars, diamonds, names, dates, and even dedications, and before her, her mother taught her as her own mother had learned it, so it was as if all the mothers and daughters were at work, all one thread interlocking and double-looping, each woman

†The *rebozo* was born in Mexico, but like all *mestizos,* it came from everywhere. It evolved from the cloths Indian women used to carry their babies, borrowed its knotted fringe from Spanish shawls, and was influenced by the silk embroideries from the imperial court of China exported to Manila, then Acapulco, via the Spanish galleons. During the colonial period, mestizo women were prohibited by statutes dictated by the Spanish Crown to dress like Indians, and since they had no means to buy clothing like the Spaniards', they began to weave cloth on the indigenous looms creating a long and narrow shawl that slowly was shaped by foreign influences. The quintessential Mexican *rebozo* is the *rebozo de bolita,* whose spotted design imitates a snakeskin, an animal venerated by the Indians in pre-Columbian times.

learning from the woman before, but adding a flourish that became her signature, then passing it on.

—Not like that, daughter, like this. It's just like braiding hair. Did you wash your hands?

—See this little spider design here, pay attention. The widow Elpidia will tell you different, but it was I who invented that.

—Hortensia, that shawl you sold the day before yesterday. Policarpa knotted the fringe, am I right? You can always tell Policarpa's work . . . it looks like she made it with her feet.

—*¡Puro cuento!* What a *mitotera* you are, Guillermina! You know I did that myself. You like weaving stories just to make trouble.

And so my grandmother as a newborn baby was wrapped within one of these famous *rebozos* of Santa María del Río, the shawls a Mexican painter claimed could serve as the national flag, the very same shawls wealthy wives coveted and stored in inlaid cedar boxes scented with apples and quinces. When my grandmother's face was still a fat cloverleaf, she was seated on a wooden crate beneath these precious *rebozos* and taught the names given each because of their color or design.

Watermelon, lantern, pearl. Rain, see, not to be confused with drizzle. Snow, dove-gray *columbino,* coral *jamoncillo.* Brown trimmed with white *coyote,* the rainbow *tornasoles,* red *quemado,* and the golden-yellow *maravilla*. See! I still remember!

Women across the republic, rich or poor, plain or beautiful, ancient or young, in the times of my grandmother all owned *rebozos*—the ones of real Chinese silk sold for prices so precious one asked for them as dowry and took them to the grave as one's burial shroud, as well as the cheap everyday variety made of cotton and bought at the market. Silk *rebozos* worn with the best dress—*de gala,* as they say. Cotton *rebozos* to carry a child, or to shoo away the flies. Devout *rebozos* to cover one's head with when entering church. Showy *rebozos* twisted and knotted in the hair with flowers and silver hair ornaments. The oldest, softest *rebozo* worn to bed. A *rebozo* as cradle, as umbrella or parasol, as basket when going to market, or modestly covering the blue-veined breast giving suck.

That world with its customs my grandmother witnessed.

Exactly!

It is only right, then, that she should have been a knotter of fringe as well, but when Soledad was still too little to braid her own hair, her mother died and left her without the language of knots and rosettes, of silk and *artisela,* of cotton and ikat-dyed secrets. There was no mother to take her hands and pass them over a dry snakeskin so her fingers would remember the patterns of diamonds.

When Guillermina departed from this world into that, she left behind an unfinished *rebozo,* the design so complex no other woman was able to finish it without undoing the threads and starting over.

—*Compadrito,* I'm sorry, I tried, but I can't. Just to undo a few inches nearly cost me my eyesight.

—Leave it like that, Ambrosio said. —Unfinished like her life.

Even with half its fringe hanging unbraided like mermaid's hair, it was an exquisite *rebozo* of five *tiras,* the cloth a beautiful blend of toffee, licorice, and vanilla stripes flecked with black and white, which is why they call this design a *caramelo.* The shawl was slippery-soft, of an excellent quality and weight, with astonishing fringe work resembling a cascade of fireworks on a field of sunflowers, but completely unsellable because of the unfinished *rapacejo.* Eventually it was forgotten, and Soledad was allowed to claim it as a plaything.

After Guillermina's sudden death, Ambrosio felt the urge to remarry. He had a child, a business, and his life ahead of him. He tied the knot with the baker's widow. But it must have been the years of black dye that seeped into Ambrosio Reyes' heart. How else to explain his dark ways? It was his new wife, a bitter woman who kneaded dough into ginger pigs, sugar shells, and buttery horns, who stole all his sweetness.

Because, to tell the truth, soon after remarrying, Ambrosio Reyes lost interest in his daughter the way one sometimes remembers the taste of a sweet but no longer longs for it. The memory was enough to satisfy him. He forgot he had once loved his Soledad, how he had enjoyed sitting with her in the doorway in a patch of sun, and how the top of her head smelled like warm chamomile tea, and this smell had made him happy. How he used to kiss a heart-shaped mole on the palm of her left hand and say, —This little mole is mine, right? How when she would ask for some *centavos* for a *chuchuluco,* he'd answer, —You are my *chuchuluco,* and pretend to gobble her up. But what most broke Soledad's heart was that he no longer asked her, —Who's my queen?

He no longer remembered—could it be? It was like the fairy tale "The Snow Queen," a bit of evil glass no bigger than a sliver had entered into his eye and heart, a tender pain that hurt when he thought about his daughter. If only he had chosen to think about her more often and dissolve that evil with tears. But Ambrosio Reyes behaved as most people do when it comes to painful thoughts. He chose not to think. And by not thinking, he allowed the memory to grow infected and more tender. How short is life and how long regret! Nothing could be done about it.

Poor Soledad. Her childhood without a childhood. She would never know what it was to have a father hold her again. There was no one to advise her, caress her, call her sweet names, soothe her, or save her. No one would touch her again with a mother's love. No soft hair across her cheek, only the soft fringe of the unfinished shawl, and now Soledad's fingers took to combing this, plaiting, unplaiting, plaiting, over and over, the language of the nervous hands. —Stop that, her stepmother would shout, but her hands never quit, even when she was sleeping.

She was thirty-three kilos of grief the day her father gave her away to her cousin in Mexico City. —It's for your own good, her father said. —You should be grateful. Of this his new wife had him convinced.

—Don't cry, Soledad. Your father is only thinking of your future. In the capital you'll have more opportunities, an education, a chance to meet a better category of people, you'll see.

So this part of the story if it were a *fotonovela* or *telenovela* could be called *Solamente Soledad* or *Sola en el mundo,* or *I'm Not to Blame,* or *What an* Historia *I've Lived.*

The unfinished *caramelo rebozo,* two dresses, and a pair of crooked shoes. This was what she was given when her father said, —Good-bye and may the Lord take care of you, and let her go to his cousin Fina's in the capital.

Soledad would remember her father's words. *Just enough, but not too much.* And though they were instructions on how to dye the black *rebozos* black, who would've guessed they would instruct her on how to live her life.

CUÍDATE

People said, —Now that you're a *señorita, cuídate.* Take care of yourself. But how was Soledad to know what they meant? *Cuídate.* Take care of yourself. Hadn't she taken care of her hair and her nails, made sure her underclothes were clean, mended her stockings, polished her shoes, washed her ears, brushed her teeth, blessed herself when she passed a church, starched and ironed her petticoat, scrubbed her armpits with a soapy cloth, dusted off the soles of her feet before getting into bed, rinsed her bloody rags in secret when she had "the rule." But they meant take care of yourself *down there.* Wasn't society strange? They demanded you not to become . . . but they didn't tell you how not to. The priest, the pope, Aunty Fina, la Señora Regina, the wise neighbor lady across the street, *las tortilleras,* the pumpkin-seed vendor, *las tamaleras,* the market women who gave her back her change with this added *pilón,* —Take care of yourself. But no one told you how to . . . well, *how* exactly.

Because wasn't a kiss part of the act of loving? In truth?

Honestly, now? Wasn't a kiss the tug of a string, a ribbon, a dance, a thread looped and interlocked that began with the lips and ended with his thing inside you. Really, there was no way once it began for her to find where or how to stop, because it was a story without beginning or end. And why was it her responsibility for her to say *enough,* when in her heart of hearts she never wanted it to end, and how sad she felt when it was over and he pulled himself away and she was just herself again, and there was nothing left of that happiness but something like the juice of the maguey, like cold spittle on her thighs, and each person went back to being just themselves.

For a little, for a moment as fine as *una espina de nopalito,* she felt as if she could never be lonely, she felt she was not herself, she was not Soledad nor was he Narciso, nor rock nor purple flower, but all rocks and purple flowers and sky and cloud and shell and pebble. It was a secret too beautiful, to tell the truth. Why had everyone kept such a marvel from her? She had not felt this well loved except perhaps when she was still inside her mother's belly, or had sat on her father's lap, the sun on the top of her head, her father's words like sunlight, —*Mi reina.* She felt when this man, this boy, this body, this Narciso put himself inside her, she was no longer a body separate from his. In that kiss, they swallowed one another, swallowed the room, the sky, the darkness, fear, and it was beautiful to feel so much a part of everything and bigger than everything. Soledad was no longer Soledad Reyes, Soledad on this earth with her two dresses, her one pair of shoes, her unfinished *caramelo rebozo,* she was not a girl anymore with sad eyes, not herself, just herself, only herself. But all things little and large, great and small, important and unassuming. A puddle of rain and the feather that fell shattering the sky inside it, the lit votive candles flickering through blue cobalt glass at the cathedral, the opening notes of that waltz without a name, a clay bowl of rice in bean broth, a steaming clod of horse dung. Everything, oh, my God, everything. A great flood, an overwhelming joy, and it was good and joyous and blessed.

SPIC SPANISH?

The old proverb was true. Spanish was the language to speak to God and English the language to talk to dogs. But Father worked for the dogs, and if they barked he had to know how to bark back. Father sent away for the Inglés Sin Stress home course in English. He practiced, when speaking to his boss, —*Gud mórning, ser.* Or meeting a woman, —*Jáu du iú du?* If asked how he was coming along with his English lessons, —*Veri uel, zanc iú.*

Because Uncle Fat-Face had been in the States longer, he gave Father advice. —Look, when speaking to police, always begin with, "Hello, my friend."

In order to advance in society, Father thought it wise to memorize several passages from the "Polite Phrases" chapter. I congratulate you. Pass on, sir. Pardon my English. I have no answer to give you. It gives me the greatest pleasure. And: I am of the same opinion.

But his English was odd to American ears. He worked at his pronunciation and tried his best to enunciate correctly. —Sir, kindly direct me to the water closet. —Please what do you say? —May I trouble you to ask for what time is? —Do me the kindness to tell me how is. When all else failed and Father couldn't make himself understood, he could resort to, —*Spic Spanish?*

Qué strange was English. Rude and to the point. No one preceded a request with a —Will you not be so kind as to do me the favor of . . . , as one ought. They just asked! Nor did they add —If God wills it to their plans, as if they were in audacious control of their own destiny. It was a barbarous language! Curt as the commands of a dog trainer. —Sit. —Speak up. And why did no one say, —You are welcome. Instead, they grunted, —Uh-huh, without looking him in the eye, and without so much as a —You are very kind, mister, and may things go well for you.

ALL PARTS FROM MEXICO, ASSEMBLED IN THE U.S.A. *OR* I AM BORN

I am the favorite child of a favorite child. I know my worth. Mother named me after a famous battle where Pancho Villa met his Waterloo.

I am the seventh born in the Reyes family of six sons. Father named them all. Rafael, Refugio, Gustavo, Alberto, Lorenzo, and Guillermo. This he did without Mother's consultation, claiming us like uncharted continents to honor the Reyes ancestors dead or dying.

Then I was born. I was a disappointment. Father had expected another boy. When I was still a spiral of sleep, he'd laugh and rub Mother's belly, bragging, —I'm going to create my own soccer team.

But he didn't laugh when he saw me. —*¡Otra vieja! Ahora, ¿cómo la voy a cuidar?*★ Mother had goofed.

—Cripes almighty! Mother said. —At least she's healthy. Here, you hold her.

Not exactly love at first sight, but a strange *déjà vu,* as if

★Tr. *Another dame! Now how am I going to take care of this one?*†

†Tr. of Tr. *How am I going to protect her from men like me?*

Father was looking into a well. The same silly face as his own, his mother's. Eyes like little houses beneath the sad roof of brow.

—Leticia. We'll name her Leticia, Father murmured.

—But I don't like that name.

—It's a good name. Leticia Reyes. Leticia. Leticia. Leticia.

And then he left. But when the nurse came to record my name, Mama heard herself say, —Celaya. A town where they'd once stopped for a mineral water and a *torta de milanesa* on a trip through Guanajuato. —Celaya, she said, surprised at her own audacity. It was the first time she disobeyed Father, but no, not the last. She reasoned the name "Leticia" belonged to some *fulana,* one of my father's "histories." —Why else would he have insisted so stubbornly?

And so I was christened Celaya, a name Father hated until his mother declared over the telephone wires, —A name pretty enough for a *telenovela.* After that, he said nothing.

Days and days, months and months. Father carried me wherever he went. I was a little fist. And then a thumb. And then I could hold my head up without letting it flop over. Father bought me crinolines, and taffeta dresses, and ribbons, and socks, and ruffled panties edged with lace, and white leather shoes soft as the ears of rabbits, and demanded I never be allowed to look raggedy. I was a cupcake. —*¿Quién te quiere?* Who loves you? he'd coo. When I burped up my milk, he was there to wipe my mouth with his Irish linen handkerchief and spit. When I began scratching and pulling my hair, he sewed flannel mittens for me that tied with pink ribbons at the wrist. When I sneezed, Father held me up to his face, and let me sneeze on him. He also learned to change my diapers, which he had never done for his sons.

I was worn on the arm like a jewel, like a bouquet of flowers, like the Infant of Prague. —My daughter, he said to the interested and uninterested. When I began to accept the bottle, Father bought one airline ticket and took me home to meet his mother. And when the Awful Grandmother saw my Father with that crazy look of joy in his eye, she knew. She was no longer his queen.

It was too late. Celaya, a town in Guanajuato where Pancho Villa met his nemesis. Celaya, the seventh child. Celaya, my father's Waterloo.

THE VOGUE

Not class like Frost Brothers, but definitely not cheese like the Kress. —Verrry rrritzy, verrry fancy, verrry Vogue, Viva says in a snooty fake accent she makes up from I don't know where. —Formals, shoes, gloves, hats, hose. Whenever you shop for a special occasion, head over to the Vogue, corner of Houston and Navarro Streets, downtown San Antonio, Viva says breathlessly as she swirls through the doors like a TV commercial.

—We're shopping for the prom, Viva says to the saleswomen trailing us. Not true, but that's how we get to play dress-up for an hour, trying on beaded gowns we can't afford. Viva pulls a purple crocheted number over her head and shimmies until it falls into place, the pearl spangles sparkling when she moves, the neckline plunging like an Acapulco cliff diver.

—Oh, my God, Viva, you look just like Cher!

The Vogue saleswomen have to wear prissy name tags that say "Miss" in front of their first names, even if they're a hundred years old! Miss Sharon, Miss Marcy, Miss Rose.

Viva asks me, —And when you're on your period, do you get real *cacosa*?

—Shit, yes!

—Ha! That's a good one. Me too.

Miss Rose hovering about, knocking on the dressing room door too sharply, and asking a hundred times, —Everything all right, honey?

—Gawd! Can't we have a little privacy here? Viva says, squeezing her *chichis* into a serve-'em-on-a-platter corset gown.

The Vogue is Viva's choice. Mine, the Woolworth's across from the Alamo because of the lunch counter that loops in and out like a snake. I like sitting next to the toothless *viejitos* enjoying their grilled tuna triangles and slurping chicken noodle soup. I could sit at that counter for hours, ordering Cokes and fries, a caramel sundae, a banana split. Or wander the aisles filling a collapsible basket with glitter nail polish, little jars of fruit-flavored lip gloss, neon felt-tip pens, take the escalator to the basement to check out the parakeets and canaries, poke around Hardware looking for cool stuff, or dig through the bargain bins for marked-down treasures.

Viva says who would ever want to shop at the Woolworth's when there's the Kress? She has a way of finding jewels even there. Like maybe picking up thick fluorescent yarn for our hair over in Knitting. Or a little girl's purse I wouldn't ever notice in a thousand years. Or the funkiest old ladies' sandals that turn sexy when she wears them.

But it's over at the Vogue that Viva's happiest. I can't see the point in spending so much time in a store that sells nothing for less than five dollars. —But who cares, says Viva. —Right? Who cares.

We try on every formal dress in the store till I complain I'm hungry. No use. Viva pauses in Jewelry and tries on a pair of gold hoop earrings almost bigger than her head.

—Gold hoops look good on us, Viva says. She means Mexicans, and who am I to argue with the fashion expert. We do look good. —Never sleep with your gold hoops, though, Viva adds. —Last time I did that I woke up and they weren't hoops anymore, but something shaped like peanuts. I'm going to write a list of twenty things you should never do, *nunca,* or you'll be sorry, and on the top of that list will be: Never, never, never sleep with your gold hoop earrings. I'm telling you.

Number two. Never date anyone prettier than yourself, Viva says, trying on a rhinestone tiara. —Believe me, I know.

She still has to pester saleswomen to help her get her hands on a felt fedora, fishnet pantyhose, pearl hair snoods, strapless bras. I'm slumped on a bench over by the elevator when she finally reappears, sighing loudly and snapping, —Number three. Never shop for more than an hour in platform shoes. My feet feel like zombies, and this place bores me to tears. Let's cut out.

—I was hoping we could stop at the Woolworth's for a chili dog, I say. —But it's late. My ma will be pissed.

—Quit already. We'll tell her . . . we were at my house bathing my mother.

Viva is braying over the genius of the story we're going to tell, exaggerating worse than ever, yakking a mile a minute when we push open the heavy glass doors of the Vogue and step out onto the busy foot traffic of Houston Street.

And then the rest, I don't remember exactly. Some big

clown in a dark suit behind us barking something, a dark shadow out of the corner of my eye, and Viva's yowl when one grabs her by the shoulder and the little one hustles me by the elbow, escorting us real quick back inside the Vogue while a bunch of shoppers stare at us, and Viva starts cussing, and me mad as hell saying, —Take your hands off her! It happens so fast I really don't know what's happening at first. Like being shaken awake from a nightmare, only the nightmare is on the wrong side.

The two guys in suits say we've stolen something. I mean, how do you like that? 'Cause we're teenagers, 'cause we're brown, 'cause we're not rich enough, right? Pisses me off. I'm thinking this as they shove us downstairs to the basement and trot us down to their offices, where there are mirrors and cameras and everything. Who the hell do they think they are? We haven't done a damn thing. Jesus Christ, lay off already, will you!

Viva is looking really scared, pathetic even, making me feel sick. I would say something to her if they'd leave us alone, but they don't let us out of their sight, not for a minute.

—Take everything out of your bags and pockets.

Viva plucks things out of her purse like she's got all the time in the world. Not me; I dump my army backpack right on the cop's desk so that all my books and papers spill out. I'm so mad I can hardly look anybody in the eye. Then I empty my pockets. I wish I had something really badass to toss on the desk, like a knife or something, but all I've got is two wads of dirty Kleenex, and my bus pass, which I flick down with as much hate as I can gather, like Billy Jack in that movie.

I wonder if they'll force us to undress, and the thought of having to undress in front of these old farts makes me pissed.

But I don't finish the thought because of what Viva tugs out of one of her pockets. A pair of gold lamé gloves, the kind that go up to your armpits, the price tag still spinning from a cotton string.

Swear to God, that's when I get really scared. Then Viva does something that's pure genius.

She starts crying.

I've never seen Viva cry, ever. Seeing her cry scares the hell out of me at first. I'm thinking maybe we should call a lawyer. There must be somebody we could call, only I can't think of anybody's name except Ralph Nader, and what good is that?

Viva begs with real tears for the store cops not to call our parents. That she's already on probation with her dad, who is Mexican Methodist and the worst, and if he finds out about this, she won't get to go to her own prom. And how she had to work after school to buy her dress, and how she only needed the gloves because she was short on cash, and she couldn't ask her dad because he didn't want her to work anyway, and go ahead, call. Her mom's dead, died from leukemia last winter, a slow, horrible death. And I don't know where she gets the nerve to make up such a bunch of baloney, but she does it, all the while sniffling and hiccuping like if every word is true. Damn, she's so good, she almost has me crying.

I don't know how, but they let us go, toss us out of there like trash bags, and we don't ask questions.

—And don't come back here.

—Don't worry, we won't.

We bust out of the double doors of the Vogue on the Navarro Street side. I mean bust out, like the Devil's on our ass. The fresh air makes me realize how hot my face is. I feel dizzy and notice this weird smell to my skin, like chlorine. I'm so relieved, I just want to break into a run, but Viva is hanging on my arm and dawdling.

—Oh, my God, Lala. You better not tell anyone. Swear to God. You promise? Promise you won't say nothing to nobody. You gotta promise.

—I promise, I say.

One minute she's scared, and the next minute I look and she's laughing with her head thrown back like a horse.

—What? I ask. —What is it? Tell me already, will you?

—Number four, never . . . , Viva begins but stops there. She's laughing so much she can't even talk.

—What? You better tell me, girl!

She pulls out of her blouse a cheap memo pad she lifted from the detective's desk.

—Shit, Viva, honest to God, you scare me.

Viva just laughs. She laughs so hard, she makes me laugh. Then I have her laughing too. We have to hold on to the building. We laugh till we're doubled over, our stomachs hurting. When we think it's finally winding down, the laughing rolls back in all over again even stronger. Viva's braying has me snorting like a pig. Till the knees give out. Till Viva has to genuflect right then and there on the sidewalk, on busy Navarro Street, I'm not kidding, and hold it in, pivoting on one foot. She's laughing so hard she can hardly talk.

Then Viva rises to her feet like an actress about to deliver her lines. For a fraction of a moment, like the eye of a camera, I catch a Viva I've never seen before, a sadness she's carried around inside her all this time, years and years and years, since she was a little kid, its silver shimmering, every bad thing that ever happened to her I see in her face, but only for a slippery second, and then it's gone. —Number four, Viva says, dead serious. —Never. Ever get arrested when . . . when you've really gotta piss.

And then it's me dropping down to the sidewalk, and Viva tottering beside me, laughing and laughing, the thin bone of an ankle wedged in our you-know-what holding back a flood, our bodies shaking, and the citizens of San Antonio walking by and thinking—*What the hell?*—and probably thinking we're crazy, and maybe we are. But who cares, right? I mean, who the hell cares?

SOMEDAY MY PRINCE POPOCATÉPETL WILL COME

—Marry someone who adores you, Mother said once. —Listen, you want a good life, make sure you're adored. Adored, you hear me? Lala, I'm talking to you. Everything else is crap, she said, ransacking the trash for the missing basket from her electric percolator. —Now where the hell did that coffee thingamajig go?

Maybe I'd met that someone who adored me. Could it be Ernesto Calderón was him? I'd had a dream about Ernesto even before I met Ernesto, and when he did appear, it was like I was trying to remember someone I already knew, someone I'd always known, even when I was floating around the Milky Way as milky dust.

Because of Father, I'm used to being adored. If somebody loves me they've got to say corny Mexican things to me, or I can't take them seriously. It makes me dizzy to hear Ernesto tell me, —Baby, if I die who will kiss you? You're my life, my eyes, my soul. I want to swallow you, masticate you, digest you, shit you.

Is that heavy or what?

So when Ernesto comes around on the very morning Mother's lecturing me on marriage, I don't know what to think. After all, maybe Ernesto Calderón is my *destino.*

—Listen up, Ernesto. You've *got* to ask my parents for their permission.

—For what?

—To marry me, silly, what else?

—Very nice. You've got it all figured out, haven't you?

I shrug, pleased with myself.

—Only you forgot one thing, Ernesto says. —You didn't ask me!

—Not with words exactly. With my body and soul.

—But don't you think we're too young to get married?

—We can be engaged till we're old enough. Lots of people do that.

—Look, don't even. I'm going to get in trouble, Ernesto says. —Forget about it.

—Don't you want to make *us* all right in the sight of God? You're the one always complaining I give you religious conflicts.

—God I can handle. It's my ma I worry about.

—Well, don't you want to?

Ernesto chews on the chain of his Virgen de Guadalupe *medalla* and looks at his sneakers. Then I hear him say, —Okay, I guess.

My heart winces, as if I'd let go a well rope, the bucket singing to the bottom. Too late. Ernesto is already on the other side of the screen door, saying hello to Mother, who's ignoring him.

I don't know why, but Mother has to choose today to experiment in the kitchen. The hottest month of the year, on the hottest dog day. Mother isn't a cook. She hardly ever cooks anything but stock Mexican ranch food—*fideo* soup, rice and beans, *carne guisada* stew, flour *tortillas.* But once in a while she gets these crazy ideas to create something new, and today is one of those onces.

When Father's truck crunches in the driveway, the house is hotter than ever, even with all the fans going. Mother's project is a foreign recipe she clipped from the pages of the *San Antonio Express-News*—chicken-fried steak—*güero* food. She spent the day preparing exotic items we could just as easily have ordered at the Luby's cafeteria—green beans with almonds, broccoli casserole, candied yams, pecan pie—but Mother swears, —Nothing beats homemade. And now here's Father blowing in like a northern wind across the plains states, swirling everything in his path.

—*¡Vieja!* My papers! Father says shouting. —Zoila, Lala, Memo, Lolo, everybody, quick! *¡Mis papeles!*

—What's happened?

—¡La Migra! Father says, meaning the Immigration. —They came to the shop today, and what do you think? Somebody told them I hire *ilegales.* Now they want proof *I'm* a citizen. Zoila, where are my discharge papers? Help me look for my papers!

When the Grandmother died, her photo and the framed Virgen de Guadalupe were moved to the living room next to the dual portrait of Presidents LBJ and Kennedy. That's when we had to stop watching television.

—To honor my mother, *vamos a guardar luto.* No television, no radio, Father had ordered. —We are in mourning.

Then he went into every room and drew all the curtains. He also covered the mirrors because that's the custom on the other side, but when we asked him why, he simply said, —Because it's proper. Maybe we weren't supposed to be thinking about how we look, or maybe he meant to keep Death from looking at us.

We lived without the jabbering of the television and radio for a while, like the house needed time to think, to remember, to think. When we talked we even lowered our voices like if we were in church. But we weren't in church. We were in *luto.*

The mirrors stayed covered for only a few days, but the curtains have been drawn tight ever since. Father's already ripping them open and filling the house with the steel-white Texas light of August. Dust swirls in the air.

—*Buenas tardes, señor.*

—Ernesto! Be of some use and help me look for my shoe box.

Father unlocks the walnut-wood armoire, dumping the contents of the drawers on the bed.

—They're coming back for me after lunch, he goes on. —Mother of the sky, help me!

Ernesto whispers to me, —Why's he looking for a shoe box?

—That's where he keeps all our important papers and stuff. Before Father inherited the walnut-wood armoire, he stashed everything in his underwear drawer. Now he stores them in a shoe box from one of his wing tips. But since we moved, well, who knows where the hell it is?

—But why would someone report you to la Migra, *señor*?

—The envy. People yellow from jealousy. How do I know, Ernesto? This is no time for talk, help me!

—Did you tell them you served in the U.S. Army, Father?

—I told, I told.

Then I imagine Father talking to the INS officers. Father's English has never been good. When he's nervous it comes out folded and creased, worse than in those old books he'd sent away for when he first came to this country and worked for Mister Dick. *How you say?*

—I told about Inchon; Pung-Pion; Fort Bragg; New Cumberland, Pennsylvania; Fort Ord; SS *Haverford Victory*; Peggy Lee, get out of here give me some money too. I even told a story.

—A story?

—How on our first trip to Tokyo we had to turn back to the Honolulu hospital when those *güeros* broke their arms and legs. You know how they like to sunbathe. They lay out on the deck, but then, what do you think? Out of nowhere the sea turned wild on us. I swear to you. A big wave came and rocked the boat like a hammock. A whole shipload of soldiers tumbled off the deck and wound up with broken arms and legs, and because of this we had to turn back. Ha, ha! What do you think la Migra said then? "We don't need stories, we need papers." Can you believe it! We don't need stories, we need papers! They even asked about your brothers, Lala. Thanks to God they were born on this side.

We turn the house upside down, but we can't find Father's shoe box. All the while Ernesto is pecking at

Father, trying to find a way in to talk about him and me, but Father keeps saying, —Later, later. Father's desperate. We find drawers stuffed with old bills, letters, class photos, drapery rings, homemade birthday cards, food coupons, rubber bands, Wilson's rabies tags, but no shoe box. Father always prides himself on being organized. In his shop, every tool, every bolt of fabric, every box of tacks is in place, a scrap swept away before it hits the floor. It drives everyone nuts. But at home, Mother's chaos rules.

—All I ask for is *one* drawer for myself, is that too much? *One* little drawer and everyone sticks their hands in here. Zoila, how many times have I told you, don't touch my things!!!

—I'm not the only one who lives here, Mother wails. —Always, always blaming me, I'm sick and tired . . .

—Sick and tired, Father parrots in English. —Sick and tired . . . disgusted!

Everything has happened so fast after the Little Grandfather's death, after the Grandmother's stroke, after packing up and leaving one city for another, and then another, burying the Grandmother, giving away her things, the quarrels, the arguments, the not speaking, the shouting, and slowly life settling down for us to begin all over again. And now this.

—My things, my things, Father says, pulling his hair and jumping up and down like a kid having a tantrum. —They're coming back after lunch!!! And he whips back the drapes in each room, opens the closets and dresser drawers, pokes under the bed.

—You're nuts, Mother says. —You act like they're going to deport you. I'll call the INS and see what's what.

Mother gets on the phone, and starts talking her English English, the English she speaks with *los güeros,* nasally and whiny with the syllables stretched out long like wet laundry on the clothesline. —*Uh. huh. Yesssss. Mmm-hhhmm. That's right.* But after a while she hangs up because they put her on hold for too long.

—Now? Ernesto asks, meaning, Should I ask him now?

—No, Ernesto, wait!

Lolo and Memo have their lawn-mowing business to worry about. With the heat, they only do hard work in the early morning or after dusk. They save the hottest part of the day for the public pool. Only Lolo is home when Father appears, and when the shoe box doesn't turn up right away, he starts worrying he'll miss his appointment at the pool.

—So your friends are more important than your father? Father says. —This is an emergency. Lolo and Ernesto, please—go look for Memo. Bring him home now!

That's how it was we're all home when the shoe box turns up.

—Here it is, Mother says, disgusted.

—But where was it?

—In the *ropero,* she says. —The walnut-wood armoire.

—But who put it there? I looked in there.

—Your mother. How do I know? It was there.

Ernesto is plucking my elbow and twitching his eyebrows. —Not now, Ernesto, I whisper.

It isn't enough, though, that the box is found. We all

have to climb in the van and accompany Father to his workshop on Nogalitos Street, even Ernesto. —Five minutes, Father says. —I promise. But after what seems like forever, when it seems Father has hauled us all to witness nothing, the INS drive up in those famous green vans. There are two officers, and what's really sad is one of them is Mexican.

—Now you see, I no lie, Father says, waving his papers. One dated the 23rd of November, 1949, said he was honorably discharged from the Armed Forces, and the other says:

> *Private Inocencio Reyes ASN 33984365 has successfully completed the Special Training Course conducted by this Unit and is graduated this twenty-first day of June 1945 at New Cumberland.*

But the one Father is proudest of is signed by the president.

—This one, Lala, you read to everybody, Father says.

—Do I *have* to?

—Read! Father orders.

REYES CASTILLO, INOCENCIO

To you who answered the call of your country and served in its Armed Forces to bring about the total defeat of the enemy, I extend the heartfelt thanks of a grateful Nation. As one of the Nation's finest, you undertook the most severe task one can be called upon to perform. Because you demonstrated the fortitude, resourcefulness and calm judgment necessary to carry out that task, we now look to you for leadership and example in further exalting our country in peace.

[signed] Harry Truman
The White House

The INS officers simply shrug and mumble, —Sorry. But sometimes it's too late for I'm sorry. Father is shaking. Instead of —No problem, my friend—which is Father's usual reply to anyone who apologizes, Father runs after them as they're getting in their van and spits, —You . . . *changos.* For you I serving this country. For what, eh? Son of a mother!

And because he can't summon the words for what he really wants to say, he says, —Get outta here . . . Make me *sick*! Then he turns around and comes back in the shop, pretending he's looking for something in the stack of fabric bolts.

We drive back home in silence, the *chicharras* droning in the pecan trees, the heat a wavy haze that rises from the asphalt like a mirage. Father looks straight ahead like a man cut out of cardboard.

When we pull up the driveway, I send Ernesto home and tell him to forget about it, forget about everything. —Tomorrow, maybe? Should I come back and ask him tomorrow?

—Just will you quit it already, Ernesto, I hiss. —Leave me alone!

Even before we open the door, there's a terrible smell

from the kitchen, worse than beans burning—Mother's home-cooked dinner! Mother has a fit. —All that work, for what? For your shit! I've had it!

It's the closest Mother's ever come to breaking down and crying, except Mother's too proud to cry. She tears off one shoe and throws it against the living room wall on top of the television set before locking herself in the bedroom. I think Mother was aiming at the Grandmother's portrait, or maybe the ones on either side, la Virgen de Guadalupe or the one of LBJ/Kennedy, I'm not sure. But the shoe strikes the wall, leaving a big black scuff mark like a comet and an indentation we have to plaster with spackle and paint over when we move.

Father scratches his head with both hands and stands in the living room blinking. The house a mess. Drawers open, couch cushions on the floor, dinner burnt and stinking, Mother locked in the bedroom. And here's Father with his shoe box, a few papers, his wooden domino box stuffed with my childhood braids, the Grandmother's toffee-striped *caramelo rebozo,* which he wraps around himself like a flag.

—Sick and tired, he says, slumping into his orange La-Z-Boy. For a long time he just sits there guarding that box of junk like the emperor Moctezuma's jewels. —My things, he keeps muttering. —You understand, don't you, Lala? Your mother . . . You *see*? You *see* what happens?

It's like when I was little. —Who do you love more, your mother or your father? I know better than to say anything.

Almost immediately after, somebody takes down the double portrait of LBJ/Kennedy. And just as soon as the *susto* is over, Father is on the telephone to anyone and everyone who will listen. Monterrey. Chicago. Philadelphia. Mexico City.

—Sister, I'm not lying to you. So there I was, it was my word against the government's . . . You don't have to believe me, brother, but this happened . . . What a barbarity! *Compadre,* who would believe this could happen to me, a veteran . . . It's an ugly story, Cuco . . . But to finish telling you the story, cousin . . . And there you have it.

And there it is.

PILÓN

Like the Mexican grocer who gives you a pilón, *something extra tossed into your bag as a thank-you for your patronage just as you are leaving, I give you here another story in thanks for having listened to my* cuento . . .

On Cinco de Mayo Street, in front of Café la Blanca, an organ grinder playing "Farolito." Out of a happy grief, people give coins for shaking awake the memory of a father, a beloved, a child whom God ran away with.

And it was as if that music stirred up things in a piece of my heart from a time I couldn't remember. From before. Not exactly a time, a feeling. The way sometimes one remembers a memory with the images blurred and rounded, but has forgotten the one thing that would draw it all into focus. In this case, I'd forgotten a mood. Not a mood—a state of being, to be more precise.

How before my body wasn't my body. I didn't have a body. I was a being as close to a spirit as a spirit. I was a ball of light floating across the planet. I mean the me I was before puberty, that red Rio Bravo you have to carry yourself over.

I don't know how it is with boys. I've never been a boy. But girls somewhere between the ages of, say, eight and puberty, girls forget they have bodies. It's the time she has trouble keeping herself clean, socks always drooping, knees pocked and bloody, hair crooked as a broom. She doesn't look in mirrors. She isn't aware of being watched. Not aware of her body causing men to look at her yet. There isn't the sense of the female body's volatility, its rude weight, the nuisance of dragging it about. There isn't the world to bully you with it, bludgeon you, condemn you to a life sentence of fear. It's the time when you look at a young girl and notice she is at her ugliest, but at the same time, at her happiest. She is a being as close to a spirit as a spirit.

Then that red Rubicon. The never going back there. To that country, I mean.

And I remember along with that feeling fluttering through the notes of "Farolito," so many things, so many, all at once, each distinct and separate, and all running together. The taste of a *caramelo* called Glorias on my tongue. At la Caleta beach, a girl with skin like *cajeta,* like goat-milk candy. The *caramelo* color of your skin after rising out of the Acapulco foam, salt water running down your hair and stinging the eyes, the raw ocean smell, and the ocean running out of your mouth and nose. My mother watering her dahlias with a hose and running a stream of water over her feet as well, Indian feet, thick and square, *como de barro,* like the red clay of Mexican pottery.

And I don't know how it is with anyone else, but for me these things, that song, that time, that place, are all bound together in a country I am homesick for, that doesn't exist anymore. That never existed. A country I invented. Like all emigrants caught between here and there.

VINTAGE BOOKS BY SANDRA CISNEROS

Caramelo

Weaving together aspects of her own life with fiction, Cisneros creates a multigenerational tale told by young Celaya "Lala" Reyes, the spirited only daughter in a Chicago family of six sons. Through summers spent visiting her grandparents in Mexico City, Lala begins to understand her place on both sides of the border. Like the cherished *rebozo,* or shawl, that has been passed down through generations of Reyes women, *Caramelo* vibrates with history, family, and love.

Fiction/0-679-74258-1 (English)/1-4000-3099-4 (Spanish)

The House on Mango Street

Told in a series of vignettes stunning for their eloquence, *The House on Mango Street* is Cisneros's now-classic novel of a young girl growing up in the Latino section of Chicago. Sometimes heartbreaking, sometimes joyous, it tells the story of Esperanza Cordero, whose neighborhood is one of harsh realities and harsh beauty, but it is a place where she can invent for herself what she will become.

Fiction/0-679-73477-5 (English)/0-679-75526-8 (Spanish)

Loose Woman

With *Loose Woman,* Sandra Cisneros gives us a vibrant collection of poems with the lilt of *Norteño* music, the ferocity of an Aztec death-goddess, and the romantic abandon

of Saturday night in a border town. By turns sensual and introspective, this is a work that is at once a tour de force and a triumphant outpouring of pure soul.
Poetry/0-679-75527-6

Woman Hollering Creek

A story collection of breathtaking range and authority, *Woman Hollering Creek* gives voice to the vibrant and varied life on both sides of the Mexican border. From a young girl revealing secrets only an eleven-year-old can know to a witch woman circling above the village on a predawn flight, the women in these stories offer tales of pure discovery, filled with moments of infinite and intimate wisdom.
Fiction/0-679-73856-8